Roadger Smith Mystery

MURDER
GOES TO
COLLEGE

by

Robert Foster

(The Author of A Merry Little Murder)

Tenth Muse Press

Library of Congress Card Catalog Number: 98-90090

In the tradition of Antohony Trollope, who in *The Warden* said, "The
Tenth Muse who now governs the peridical press."

Tenth Muse Press
491 Hubbard Ave.
Elgin, IL 60123

Printed in the USA by

MORRIS PUBLISHING

3212 East Highway 30 • Kearney, NE 68847 • 1-800-650-7888

For Jane and Willie

IMPERTINENCE FROM THE AUTHOR:

Statements in this volume pertaining to specific books are true, particularly in regard to the history of the publication of Jefferson's *The Life and Morals of Jesus of Nazareth* and variances in the first and second editions of *The Scarlet Letter*. Mark Twain's "The Question" is a thinly disguised allusion to another Twain work and to the man who discovered it. All references, however, to Wade Watts' *The Hill* are pure frumery. The monetary amounts for the various books presented have no credence, as books, like antiques and reputations, have value only in so far as a particular individual wishes.

MURDER GOES TO COLLEGE

CHAPTER I

HOLY THURSDAY

The trumpet of a prophecy! O wind,
If winter comes, can spring be far behind.
"Ode to the West Wind,"
                                        Percy Bysshe Shelley

There are two good ways to get into Walden, Missouri, if you happen to be a cow. You can take a cattle car on the CC and B Railroad up the tracks or down the tracks, or you can ride in a cattle truck up Route 61 or down Route 61. Passenger service on the CC and B to Walden was discontinued after the flood of '87 so humans, unlike bovines, have no choice. From St. Louis or even Kansas City the trip is rather pleasant, with good highways, often four lane. From Chicago or its suburbs, like Oak Meadow, however, the drive has many disadvantages. The distance is great (over three hundred miles), too short for an overnight stop but too long for a pleasure trip. The route is convolutional, requiring many different highways. The roads are often not only two lane but better engineered as bicycle paths than as state highways. This may have been the intention when the roads were built way back in the Gay Nineties, a term gone out of use in recent years.

Bernadine and Blanche Badger were good travelers, however, and not only took the bumps and sharp turns in stride but actually enjoyed the trip, like two young school girls being taken for a Sunday afternoon drive by a gentleman caller, shades of an Emily Dickinson poem. Their driver on this occasion was far from being a gentleman caller, however. In fact, she was no gentleman at all. She answered to the name of Mary Mallony, newly widowed in a murder that shook the Chicago area legal profession over the past winter. Bernadine and Blanche Badger along with their great nephew, John Badger Smith, had no small part in bringing that crime to a quick resolution. The two ladies were on their way to visit their great-nephew on the campus of Carlton-Stokes College, on the western edge of Walden, MO. John Badger Smith, known to all his friends and enemies alike as Badger, but to his great aunts as Johnny, taught English at the college and had prevailed upon his favorite relatives to come down for a visit over the spring break at Easter time.

"Why can't you just drive up to Oak Meadow the way you always do?" asked Blanche, when Badger first mentioned the idea while he was visiting at Christmas. "After all, we don't have a car and there is no plane, train, or bus service." (There actually was bus service, but it was irregular at best, and only reached best about once a year, in the middle of the winter when all of the smells accumulating all summer were flushed from the cabin by the noisy but very effective heating system. That none of the cattle took the bus attests to its lack of amenities.)

"Two reasons," said Badger. "It is spring break for the students, but not for me. I have to be at the college to take charge of all those eager young scholars who remain on campus because they live too far away to go home for the short break. This is one of the little responsibilities that came with my job. Last year it was

Prof. Aquino's task; this year it's mine. Besides, I want to show you the school. It's really the most beautiful campus you'll ever see. And . . . ., if you stay until after Easter you can sit in on some of my classes. I'd love to show off for you, and show you off to some of my students."

"We would love to visit your school, Johnny," said Bernadine, "but how do you propose we get all the way to Walden, Missouri, hitch-hike?"

"That would be easy enough for me," broke in Blanche, "I'm only seventy-six, but Bernadine might have a little trouble. She's pushing eighty-three you know."

"Yes, but my legs are better. I wouldn't have to walk; I'd just lift my skirt like Claudette Colbert and I'd get an Alan Hale to stop in a great hurry."

Badger had smiled, not only at his aunts' bit of whimsy but also at the opportunity to reveal his master plan. "No, I wouldn't want either of you to tramp down the highway, although it would be a wondrous sight. Why couldn't you get Mary to drive you? You could all stay at the student union free of charge. One of my faculty fringe benefits is free accommodations for my guests a few times a year. The rooms are comfortable and clean, and it is very hard to beat the price."

"So that's it!" teased Blanche. "You just wish to show off for Mary, not your old maid aunts. A fine thing!"

After feigning disappointment the two hugged their nephew and promised to try their best to talk

Mary into the Easter trip, not realizing what an easy
task that would turn out to be.

The car, a year old Lincoln Continental bought
by Mary's now deceased husband, came to a halt at
the only stop light in Walden. The buildings were all
two story and very simple in architecture but had a
beauty that grew out of function and maintenance.
The late afternoon sun played black magic with the
structures and cast dark shadows that highlighted
the solar streaks between the buildings.

When the light changed they drove down one
block to where a large billboard sign announced the
way to Carlton-Stokes College. Although they didn't
know it at the time, it also pointed to a long week-end of
mystery and murder. Mary turned right and followed
the road as it outlined houses and then rose sharply up
a steep hill and wound around the first campus
buildings, all red brick with imposing Greek columns.
Although the Chicago area was technically into the
spring season, the ground, when the three left that
morning, had been hard and brown, and the North
Wind retained the smell of snow that any Chicagoan
could identify. Walden, unlike Chicago, had not only
the calendar of spring but the weather as well. The
grass was green and the trees were budding. The
dense white cherry blossoms, however, made the
whole area appear almost like winter. Yellow and
red tulips outlined many of the sidewalks close to the
campus buildings.

Mary pulled the Lincoln into a parking space in
a small black-topped, almost empty, parking lot at what
appeared to be the highest point on the campus. She
got out of the car and stretched, allowing any early
robins who happened to be flying by to see the skirt of

her one piece, rich brown dress blowing in the light wind. He (or she, as robins are so often ladies) would also see that Mary's hair almost matched the dress. Bernadine rose from the passenger seat slowly, favoring her arthritic back that no one was supposed to notice. Her dark blue dress wrapped around her legs and girlishly slim body rather than blow in the wind, and her hair was more the color of bitter chocolate than rich brown. At age eighty-two no silver threads had yet dared to streak her temples. Blanche did not step or get out of the car. She didn't even alight. She bounded. It was as though she had been propelled from the mouth of a canon like puffed rice. She also wore a blue dress, one that matched the pill box hat that perched on her head, a head that was not rich brown or even bitter chocolate but rather an indescribable color, both brown and gray without quite being either. Once out of the car she looked around the campus, then nodded at a building slightly below them, the back of which they had passed on their way up the Hill. (It was never the *hill.*)

"That's where we'll find Johnny," she said.

"How can you be so sure? asked Bernadine.

"After working in libraries for most of my life I can identify one anywhere, and Johnny said he would be in the library all afternoon. I'm surprised you didn't see for yourself. You were a librarian longer than I."

Mary smiled to herself, as she was sure that Blanche had seen the small arrow sign on the road saying, "Library Loading Dock."

They left everything in the spacious Lincoln except for their purses, of course, and walked down the sidewalk to the front of the library building, where a bronze plaque on the side of the double doors identified the building as the Carl Bach Library, erected in 1949. The three entered and climbed the half dozen steps to the first floor. On their left a sign on a door identified it as the entrance to the office of the president. On their right a door was marked "Treasurer's Office," so this was both the library and administration building. Both offices appeared closed and locked, with no light shining through the frosted windows or bleeding out under the doors. Another bronze plaque pointed to the second story and said "Library." The three climbed the stairs to the landing and the next floor.

Both of the Badger sisters smiled when they turned to face the floor above. There was no doubt as to where they were heading. Moslems have their Mecca, Jews their Wailing Wall, and Christians their Golgotha, but these are as nothing compared to book lovers and their libraries. As they stepped through the glass door they became Dorothy and Toto stepping out of the forest with the Emerald City just before them. One could almost hear the Harold Arlen music.

The large room was almost deserted. A student was sitting behind the main desk typing at a computer. Acting like the man in charge, he looked up and scowled any time he heard so much as a cough. The front of the desk was decorated with a computer banner with a large bunny on each side and large lettering in the middle proclaiming "Happy Easter!"

Two young men were playing chess at one of the tables and several girls were reading at another along one wall. An attractive couple had found a back cubicle ideal for holding hands and occasionally whispering and kissing.

"You're here!" A deep bass voice filled the room and made heads snap up and turn about. A short, stoop shouldered man in his late thirties stepped out from among rows of bookcases in a section identified in every library as "The Stacks." Without embarrassment or concern that he was speaking above a whisper in a library, the eighth deadly sin, Badger Smith, for this could be no one else, ran out to Bernadine and Blanche and hugged and kissed them, to their delight. One of the chess players, a member of Badger's three o'clock class in composition, was now being made aware for the first time that Mr. Smith was indeed human. Embarrassment did, however, come to Badger when he released his aunts and then looked at Mary. She stepped up and placed her cheek for Badger to kiss, which he did with a great deal of self-conscious pleasure. Without further words he led the three women into a small conference room and closed the door before seating them around a large table. His light brown slacks blended in with the vinyl seat covering as he plopped into a chair. A camel hair sport coat which was almost the color of his own now thinning tonsorial splendor hung on his frame, hung because of the weight of books in the pockets. He wore a blue shirt open at the neck. A pair of penny loafers partially concealed his brown and blue socks, one of each.

"It's almost four-thirty," said Badger. "I was beginning to get worried. Did you have any trouble?"

"None at all," said Mary. "We went to eight o'clock mass this morning so we didn't get started until after nine. Then we stopped at a lovely little church and later dawdled a bit over lunch, I'm afraid."

"Today is Holy Thursday," said Blanche. "There is a partial indulgence for each church visited."

"I'm afraid there is little time to visit our local church today. This won't exactly be the vacation I had planned. Something has happened on campus, and because I'm in charge of things over the spring break I am very much involved," Badger forlornly explained.

" 'The best-laid schemes o' Mice and Men / Gang aft a-gley,'" quoted Blanche, not only a lover of Robert Burns but of all good poetry. "What's the matter? Is there something we can do?"

"I really don't see how," said Badger. "Some valuable books apparently are missing from our Archives. Our head librarian thinks that they may have been stolen."

This announcement took ten years apiece off of Bernadine and Blanche's looks, and Mary's pretty face flushed. Books...stolen...head librarian...mystery! This might turn out to be a perfect vacation. After all, who knew books better than Bernadine and Blanche? Blanche had been librarian and head librarian in a Chicago branch for close to forty years, while Bernadine had been librarian, head librarian and regional librarian for almost a decade longer. If there were anything they did not know about books it would have to be in the realm of horse racing. And Mary? Well Mary was a heavy reader who, since Christmas, had been doing volunteer work with the Badger sisters at the St. Edward's School library back in Oak Meadow and had learned a great deal, under expert tutelage.

"I think we could be a great help to you," said

Bernadine. "We did spend a few days inside a library and learned a thing or two about tomes. Give us the details."

"I'd love to," said Badger, "but I really don't know very much as yet. I received a phone call today from my best friend on campus, George. He is on the Archives committee and had just received a call from Graham Carruth, our head librarian. George thinks he said that our first edition copy of *The Scarlet Letter* was missing. Graham apparently wasn't very clear. George thinks he wants all of the members of the committee who are in town to meet with him tonight here in the library. Graham is supposedly bringing in some experts from who knows where. Because I'm the only staff member here on campus in an official capacity I am requested to be here also, and requested is merely a polite term for ordered."

"What time is this meeting and is it going to be here?" asked Blanche.

"Eight o'clock over there in the Archives."

"Good," said Bernadine. "That gives us just enough time to check into our rooms at the student union, get down to your apartment for some libations, that is if you have any refreshments for your tired old aunts and Mary, get a bite to eat at one of your elegant local dining spots, and get back up here for the meeting."

Blanche smiled. "I am quite sure that your head librarian, what was it you said his name was? I do take after my nephew; I can never remember names." She looked at Mary.

"Graham Carruth."

"Yes, Graham Carruth, won't mind three extra people at the meeting. You have our permission to tell him you have brought in your own experts. I was once on a committee that accepted a first edition of *The Scarlet Letter* for the Chicago Public Library from the late Patrick Werner estate. You remember, Bernadine, the library had no proper place to keep it at the time so I brought it home for over two weeks. You can learn a great deal about a book in two weeks, especially if it is a book you already love."

"I'm sure that Graham will be very pleased to have you three experts at the meeting, and if he isn't he'll have you anyway, if you really want to come," Badger said with a good deal of enjoyment. "I will have to modify your plan slightly, however, Bernadine. We will, indeed, check you in at the student union and get us a drink or two at my place, but we won't be going out. We'll eat at my apartment."

"Oh, that would be much too much trouble!" Bernadine almost shouted.

"Don't worry. You won't have to eat my cooking. My friend, George, is at my place now, preparing our dinner. He is, unlike your nephew, an excellent cook. He is also a very good friend and close companion. You'll like him." Badger turned now to Mary and seemed to be talking only to her. "When I came here George was my first friend. He showed me the ropes. Even in a small school like Carlton-Stokes there are a number of pit falls, and it is very reassuring to have one of those ropes handy to climb out of the pit if it is ever necessary, as it has been a few more times than I would really like to admit to anyone. His name is George Mercater as in Mercater's scale."

The four left the conference room and headed for the library door and the stairs. Bernadine holding one of Badger's arms more for love than the support her tired back needed. Blanche and Mary led the way, a thirty-six year old and a seventy-six year old showing the now departing students what the word "sprightly" means.

The ride to the student union was short and uneventful, taking almost longer to embark and disembark than to drive. The union itself was at first a disappointment to the three women, as they entered it from a side door. It was one of the oldest buildings on the campus and at one time apparently had acted as administration building, a classroom building, and auditorium, all at the same time. A plaque above one door said, Harriet Lueker Hall, 1883. The inside of the building was another matter. It had been completely renovated, with the top floor of the building devoted to faculty office space and small classrooms for the English department. A bookstore, closed over vacation, occupied most of the basement. The floor they came in on contained the lobby, the ten bedroom hotel and a few offices. To one side was a brightly decorated room with large booths and a counter that looked like a soda fountain of an age passed. Over the entrance way hung a sign announcing "The Lion's Den." Taped to the closed door was a piece of paper identifying the hours: "Open 7 A.M. to 5 P.M. during Spring Vacation."

"I take it from that sign that the your school mascot is a lion, unless you have more than one student union." said Mary.

"Yes, but students didn't name the room," explained Badger. "That was one of the trusties. There is a smaller version of this in the basement of the library that the students named 'The Lion's Pause,' spelled P-A-U-S-E. If you want coffee over there you ask for an Androcles. In "The Lion's Den" you just ask for coffee. Unfortunately, 'The Lion's Pause' is closed all this week. We'll have to eat breakfast here."

" 'And dar'st thou then, / To beard the lion in his den?' A bit of 'Lochinvar,' " said Blanche. .

Badger led them up to the check-in counter, carrying the small bag that held Bernadine's and Blanche's clothing. Mary carried her own. He then helped them to their rooms, one for his aunts and one for Mary, side by side, or adjoining as they say in the trade.

Badger waited by the desk and listened to the student clerk talk to his girl friend on the phone. The ladies spent little time with their luggage, so they were back outside and in Mary's car in just a few minutes.

"I'll drive you to your car, Badger, if you'll tell me how to get to it," said Mary.

"I didn't take my car up the Hill this morning ," said Badger. "Once spring comes to Walden I walk just as much as I can. So I'll just point the way and we can go directly to my apartment. Just follow this road and I'll tell you where to turn."

Mary followed Badger's directions, as she did a good many more times over this Easter week-end.

❀   ❀   ❀

CHAPTER II

EARLY EVENING HOLY THURSDAY

Spring rides no horses down the Hill,
But comes on foot, a goose-girl still
And all the loveliest things there be
Come simply so, it seems to me.
    "The Goose-Girl,"   Edna St. Vincent Millay

They were soon in front of a two story house that was just one block over from where the three women had halted at the stop sign a little over an hour before. They all recognized Badger's Ford Taurus parked vertically in front of the house, almost up to the sidewalk, there being no curbing to obstruct any cars. A large red maple, newly decked out in leaves, was waving a greeting in the gentle spring breeze. Badger led the way through the center door and up the stairs that cut the building in half. When he reached the landing and took a ninety degree turn he called "George, George, we're here," and continued up the remaining steps.

George, a tall, slightly stooped man in his mid forties stepped out of the door on Badger's left. He wore slacks, shirt and pullover sweater; however most of his clothing was hidden by a large green and white apron. He waved a spatula.

"Happy Easter, Bernadine! Happy Easter, Blanche! Happy Easter, Mary! Come in, come in." He pushed Badger through the door then kissed each of the ladies as she reached the top step, acting not only as if he had known them all for twenty years but as if he were the occupant of the apartment. "Sit down, sit down. I'll get Badger to make us some drinks before you sit down to Chicken ala Mercater."

Bernadine was noticeably out of breath as she walked into the small room, divided by a long, four foot high bookcase in order to make two areas, a living room and a kitchen. Books were jammed into the case in every manner possible. The top had several stacks of books that appeared to be ready to fall into the kitchen, a situation worsened when Badger unloaded his pockets. On the living room side was a short couch next to the door, a tall lamp, a coffee table, two small chairs, and a table made from an old fashioned orange crate covered with oil cloth. This sat below a window, also draped in oil cloth, that looked out over the two cars and a small park beyond. By the far wall was a gas space heater under a television table and t.v. The heater was hidden by a piece of stained plywood decorated with two horse head plaques. Next to it, in the corner, rested a double bass violin, looking somehow like an ineffectual scarecrow. The top of the t.v. was filled with sheets of music held down by a German bow and a tin of rosin. On the kitchen side were a two burner stove, a refrigerator old enough to be called an ice box, and a sink and counter with an almost new microwave oven incongruously perched on it. Above it hung two very old cabinets that appeared to have been taken from a burned out building. A kitchen table and two chairs next to the only other window completed the furnishings. The walls were filled with paintings, color prints, and sketches, from Titian to Bellows to Badger. Somehow the total result was not altogether displeasing. The room had warmth and an old shoe sort of comfort.

"Where do you sleep, Johnny?" asked Bernadine.

"Who is Johnny?" called a confused George from the kitchen.

"Johnny is that good looking man standing next to you, fixing drinks. He gets his looks from his Great Aunt Bernadine. Blanche and I claim the right to call him by a diminutive of his first name. After all, you can't expect us to call him by our *last* name, now can you?"

"I see," said George. "Well, Johnny has a . . . ouch! Okay, I get it! Badger has a bedroom, closet, and degree of indoor plumbing just across the hall," called George from the other side of the bookcase, as he went back to stirring mushrooms into his chicken dish and adding a bit more than just a dash of salt.

The Badger sisters sat primly on the worn and somewhat dusty couch and Mary took the chair closest to the bookcase. Badger and George constantly bumped one another in the kitchen until Badger emerged with a pitcher of dry Manhattans for his aunts and Mary and Martinis on the rocks for George and himself. George followed with a plate of cheese and crackers, placing it on the coffee table and then sat in the chair by the window. Badger carried a straight chair in from the kitchen area and placed it close to Mary. He poured the drinks for the three women then sat.

"Since we disposed of most of the small talk between your library and here," said Bernadine, "I propose that we get down to the business of the missing Hawthorne book. Mr. Mercater, would you go over what you know?" She held up a cigarette for Badger to light, which he did with a flick of his lighter then waited for Blanche to draw a cigarette from her silver case, which he also lit. With these two smoking was not so much a habit as it was a ritual. Bernadine and Blanche had been smoking ever since they were in college. Neither one inhaled, which filled the room with a great deal more smoke than if they had.

"Certainly," said George, "provided you will all call me by my first name, which is George, after my father."

"Well, George, one of our favorite names, by the way, we are all very anxious to get into this mystery, if you can help us."

George looked slightly puzzled but always enjoyed having the floor, especially around Badger. "I'm very surprised that you know anything about the case, having just arrived in Walden. The situation is this: Graham Carruth, the head librarian - actually he is the only full time librarian at the college - called me this morning about ten o'clock and said that our first edition of Hawthorne's *The Scarlet Letter* was missing. I think he said something about a forgery in its place, but I'm not sure. When Graham is excited he is very difficult to understand."

"A forgery, of *The Scarlet Letter* !" said Blanche. "That would be a very difficult feat to manage."

"Yes, I suppose so," said George. "At any rate, that is what I think he said. He did add that all of the members of the Archives committee who were in town were to meet in the library at eight o'clock tonight . . . along with several book collectors who live in the general area. He wants their help. Graham acts as though he is in charge but he is really a very insecure person at times."

"Why would it be difficult to forge the book?" asked Badger. "Just find an old copy of it and change the back of the title page. With all the inks and computer helps, I would think forgery of books would be an easy task. Look at all the counterfeit money being passed around everywhere you go, even some in Walden about a year ago. Some high school kids made ten dollar bills on their computer."

"With many of the newer books that would be true, but you are forgetting a few things, Johnny," said Blanche. Anyone interested in a first edition of *The Scarlet Letter* would have checked on type and color of binding and the changes in the text and would recognize a substitute. The first edition had no preface, but all of the subsequent editions did. Ripping out the pages wouldn't work. One would be able to see where they had been. Then there were many changes in the text. The mistakes made in the first edition were corrected in the second. Book writing and publishing are done by brilliant people who work for a perfect product, but there always seem to be flaws. It seems nothing is perfect. Even Heaven had its Lucifer."

"You are, of course, right, Blanche," admitted Badger. "I often find mistakes in books and magazines. I guess they would be hard to hide. Maybe we'll learn a little more from the experts. Any idea, George, who those helpers Graham has invited might be?"

"I'm not positive, but I think I can make a pretty good guess. I'm sure that Gary Jurgenson would be one of them. He runs a printing company down in Hannibal," George told the ladies. "Badger knows him. He published Badger's book of poems, not that that made him rich. He makes his money on calendars, business brochures, and things of that sort. He does all the catalogs for the college and many of the schools in this general area."

"Right," said Badger. "He has quite an impressive collection of first editions and autographed books in glass cabinets in his waiting room. He has an autographed, first edition of Faulkner's *Intruder in the Dust* that I'd give an extra large pitcher of Martinis for. Who else?"

"Oh, thank you, Johnny. That's so much nicer than what Mr. Garner would have given for the vice-presidentsy." said Bernadine.

"Jack Zinecor over at Goodman College in Quincy would be another good guess, pun not intended. I doubt if you even know him, Badger. He teaches romance languages." He turned to Bernadine. "The same as I do, so I see him at conferences. Like us, he's not married so he spends what money he has on first editions, mainly of the one and two hundred dollar variety. He makes a little extra writing translations. Does about the best job on the Existentialists that we have in American English. He's done half a dozen of them. They sell well on the West Coast. Then, I'd say that Dennis Marlin seems a logical choice, since he's right here in Walden."

"Yes, of course," Badger set down his glass and lit a cigarette then looked at his aunts. "Marlin is something of an incongruity. He's a Harvard graduate and gentleman farmer living on the edge of Walden on just a few hundred acres."

"Surely a Harvard graduate isn't that unusual in a college community," said Mary.

"Certainly not," broke in George, "Dr. Ford, the dean of the faculty, has his D.D. from Harvard, and Doug Steensland in our music department is a Yale man, but you don't find many Ivy Leaguers out with the corn and soy beans, not that he spends much time in the fields."

"I think I told you about him one time," said Badger. "He travels all over the world buying art treasures and books. You can go into almost any museum in the Midwest and see something tagged 'On special loan from the collection of Mr. and Mrs. Dennis Marlin.'"

"Corn and soy beans must bring very high prices in Missouri!" said Mary.

"He made all his money investing in real estate. There is some talk that he was one of those who made big money on the S. and L. scandal a few years back," said George. "Badger, I'll take another of your Martinis. Marlin doesn't show off his collection of first editions the way Gary Jurgenson does. Marlin keeps his all locked away somewhere. He comes around our library quite often checking on books. He does know the subject."

Badger had gotten up to refresh George's drink as well as his own and had taken the Manhattan pitcher with him to save time. He looked over the book case from the kitchen. "What about that strange one who lives on the bluff south of town. The one in the antebellum home overlooking the river?"

George smiled. "Oh yes, Master James Craig. You never met him, did you Badger?" He didn't wait for Badger to answer. "His home isn't antebellum unless the term now refers to before World War II. He bought the house a few years before you came here and redid the facade to resemble a mansion in the Old South. His wealth and interest in books he inherited from his father, a rather well known Missouri politician in the Kansas City area."

Badger reentered with the drinks and everyone was silent as if there were something sacred about the cocktail ritual, as indeed there was. After he had poured the drinks he took his lighter and waited for his aunts to produce cigarettes, then lit them. Mary and George were the non-smokers in the room. The smoke danced by them and exited stage right at the partly opened window.

Blanche struck a schoolgirl pose. "What was it Fran Lebowitz said about cigarettes? 'Smoking is, as far as I am concerned, the entire point of being an adult.'" She then stuck out her tongue at no one in particular.

"Well, I'd say, getting back to the subject, that we have quite a motley crew in this stormy sea," said Bernadine "Anyone else?"

"No one I can think of," said George. "Of course, there are the Archives committee members. All of us are some sort of experts, or think we are, in our own way and within certain limited categories. Everyone on the committee has learned a great deal about rare books." He turned his attention to Mary and the

Badger sisters. "You see, Carlton-Stokes College has one of the very best collections of American first editions and rare books in the country, if not *the* best, all because we have our church's national Archives on the campus."

"Yes, Blanche and I have had occasion to contact Carlton-Stokes on a number of issues regarding rare books," said Bernadine.

"I assume that we'll get to meet most of the Archives committee members at tonight's gathering," said Blanche.

"You coming? Wonderful!" said George. "This should shake up a few people!"

"But we really don't want to cause any bother," said Mary.

"Now, don't be a goose-girl, Mary. Of course you want to cause some bother. Don't worry," said George. "Graham is a good man but tends to be a bit stuffy. No, not a bit stuffy, a great deal stuffy. He wants to have everything his own way then gets terribly flustered when he does, and decidedly irritated when he doesn't. You ladies will irritate him like sand in an oyster."

"Maybe," said Blanche, "it will bring out a few pearls."

"There is no doubt that it will. Badger, you told me that I would like your aunts and Mary, and you certainly were correct in that. This is going to be an Easter I will long remember," said George.

❀   ❀   ❀

CHAPTER III

HOLY THURSDAY EVENING

in Just-
spring when the world is mud-
luscious the little
lame balloonman
whistles far and wee
　　　　"Chansons Innocentes,"　e. e. cummings

They had finished cocktails and had entertained one another with talk of many things, yes, from cabbages to kings. George's salad and Chicken ala Mercater had been a great success even though they had had to eat in the living room, as there were insufficient chairs at the kitchen table. George had willingly promised to write down the recipe for Bernadine and Mary. Dessert and coffee had been put off until later, as time was running short. Mary's Lincoln was quite large enough to accommodate the five, and they arrived at the library desk just as the large clock on the end of one of the stacks proclaimed eight o'clock with a faint click.

This time when the five climbed the stairs and entered the Carl Bach Memorial Library the complete group came out of the woods - Dorothy, Toto, Scarecrow, Woodsman, and Lion. The reader will have to decide which was which. They were on their way to the Emerald City, not in search of the Wizard but a mystery that had all the anticipated pleasure of a fresh crossword puzzle, a newly discovered Shakespearean tragedy, or an evening with the Chicago Symphony. Bernadine and Blanche were thinking of old books and all of the beautiful enigmas they presented. Badger had his mind on crime and another chance to exercise his powers of logic not to mention the chance to impress Mary Mallony. Mary was excited at the prospect not only of being impressed by Badger but of possibly impressing him with her own intelligence, of which she had considerable but had not shown. And what of George? He just couldn't wait to see Graham Carruth's reaction to the three guests, two of whom knew more about books than the librarian himself, if Badger had been telling him the truth about Bernadine and Blanche, and Badger never lied, at least not to George. More importantly, if the irritation failed to bring out even one pearl, there was no question that the meeting would bring out at least a bit of Coral, Coral Reiser.

"Where have you been? All of the other members of the committee are already here and ready to start," said a tall, balding man in his early sixties, stepping out from the stacks. He glared at the three women. His voice had all the power and force that his powerful physique suggested. "I'm sorry but the library is closed. I was just going to lock the door."

"These are my week-end guests, Graham. My two great aunts, Bernadine and Blanche Badger, and their neighbor and a special friend, Mary Mallony. I thought they might be of special help as my aunts worked in the Chicago Public Library system for a good many years. And, it is eight o'clock on the dot. We are on time; all the others were early."

"I'm very pleased to know you," Graham Carruth said to the three women, though his face said that he certainly was not. "I don't know if there will be enough space for three extras in the Archives room where we are meeting."

"We'll find a way to squeeze them in," said George. "I'll lock the door. You show the ladies to the room." He walked back to the door as Graham led the way through the stacks to a large room from which a good deal of verbal noise was emanating.

All talking stopped as the new arrivals entered the room. A number of people were seated at a large old, oak conference table, dwarfed by cases and cabinets around the four walls filled with books and documents. A closed door at the far end added a degree of mystery to the room, that despite its bright fluorescent ceiling lights always reminded Badger of a mausoleum.

"These are my aunts from Oak Meadow, Illinois, both retired librarians, and a friend of ours, Mary Mallony, who is an expert on Hawthorne," he lied without shame but with a degree of pleasure. I have asked them here this evening because they know a great deal about libraries and the books that fill them." He looked about the room at all who were there.

Badger, who had the world's worst memory for names, was glad that he did not have to introduce the faculty members. A man who looked as though he might have been George Washington in an earlier life stood up, leaning lightly on a cane with a silver handle, ornately carved with religious symbols, a gift from his congregation.

"I am Dr. Karl Lehr, pastor of the Church of

Redemption here in Walden. I'm the outsider on the committee." There were few people in Walden who referred to themselves as doctor, although many had the degree on campus. Dr. Lehr was one of those exceptions, an exception that everyone respected. He smiled and took a seat.

"I'm Edmund Linehan," said a very tall gray haired man, who stood when Dr. Lehr sat down. "I represent the history department, or social studies, for the literal minded. Marv Elbert, the chairman, normally would be here, but he's chasing rainbows this week." He had a twinkle in his eye, an integral part of his distinguished face.

The next to stand was a short Hispanic man with black hair and a grin as warming as Edmund Linehan's eye. "I am Onorio Flores and I not only represent the graphics arts department, I am it, or as Pogo said, 'We have met the enemy and they are us.'"

"Everyone calls him Charlie," said George.

"I like Onorio," said Bernadine. "Such a lovely old name."

"Coral Reiser," said an attractive lady about Mary's age, who remained seated. "I'm in the music department, piano, harmony, and music history."

On the other side of the table sat four men. None made a move to stand or even identify himself. Graham Carruth stepped forward and addressed not only the new arrivals but the entire group. "These four men were brought in by me to go over the entire Archives, not only this room but those two rooms beyond that door." He pointed to the mysterious door. He nodded his head at each as he named the four, starting at the far end of the room. "Mr. Dennis Marlin, Mr. Gary Jurgenson, Mr. John Zinecor, and Mr. James Craig." Each of the four nodded back as his name was pronounced. "Of course Prof. Mercater is here representing the language department and I asked Prof. Smith in because he is the President's representative during the vacation and I think it best to have a member of the English department here anyway since Ken Ettner is out of town."

Dr. Lehr, by waving his hand, encouraged his side of the table to move down, making room for three more. He pulled some chairs from against the bookcase and motioned for the ladies to sit, which they did with Mary at one corner. Graham sat down at the head of the table and George moved quickly down the table to the end and pulled up a chair next to Coral Reiser, who gave him a special smile. Badger walked to the foot and took a seat on the end, so that George was on his right and Dennis Marlin on his left.

Although it is and always has been a general rule that smoking is not permitted in a library and certainly not in an archives filled with valuable rare books and documents, Dennis Marlin had an ash tray in front of him with several cigarette butts and an abundance of ashes. It was almost hidden from view by all of the books and papers on the table. As Graham began his monologue, Marlin lit another cigarette, blowing the smoke out of the side of his mouth. There are always privileges for those who take without asking, even in a college as academically centered as Carlton-Stokes. There are always exceptions that test any rule, any rule at all.

"Gentlemen . . . and ladies, our first edition of*The*

Scarlet Letter has been stolen," Graham began. "I discovered it quite by accident when I went to check on a question Mr. Jurgenson here had about Sandburg's *The people, Yes.* When I found the Hawthorne book missing I . . . . ."

"Wait a minute," said Badger. "Let's try to keep things in order. How did checking on a question on *The People, Yes* lead you to discover that *The Scarlet Letter* was missing? And why do you insist on saying that the book was stolen when it is only missing?"

"I guess I'm not telling it very well," said Graham, whose black suit and conservative tie made Badger think of Pluto's helper, an appropriate simile considering the ossuary they were in. "I'll try to speak more slowly. As I was saying, I came to the Archives to check on a question Mr. Jurgenson had about the Sandburg book. We have a first edition, signed copy of every one of Carl Sandburg's books published in his lifetime *The People, Yes* was the handsomest tome of the lot. It was in mint condition, or as we might say, press condition. It was not in its place. I looked, but I couldn't find it anywhere."

"Couldn't it have been checked out?" asked Coral Reiser, "I know I checked out our facsimile copy of Schoenberg's *Pierrot Lunaire* just a few days ago . . . That's not missing, is it?" George smiled at the perfection of Miss Reiser's French pronunciation.

"No, Miss Reiser," said Graham. "Our music library is intact. I examined the sign-out sheet the first thing. Besides, only faculty members are allowed to take items from the Archives and they are not supposed to leave the building with them. Nothing by Sandburg has been signed out since last month when Badger checked out *The People, Yes*, and I was here when he checked it back in an hour later. At any rate, I noticed in looking over the shelves that all the books in the H section were slightly dusty except *The Scarlet Letter*, so I pulled the book out and glanced through it. Someone had very cleverly taken a second edition and made it look like a first. The wording on the back of the title page has been very carefully changed with India ink." He picked up a book and waved it around. No one was really close enough or quick enough to see any changes or even to tell if it was indeed*The Scarlet Letter* he was waving."

"I can't imagine anyone who has access to this room doing such a thing," said Gary Jurgenson, "but I saw the book. It was done, all right."

"If you look closely you can see where two pages were cut from the book, and the page numbers have been altered in the preliminary section to end with Roman numeral four rather than six. This helped to compensate for the two page preface in the second edition; the first had no preface. This forgery might have gone undetected for years had I not been alarmed by the missing Sandburg book."

"Are you absolutely sure of this, Graham?" asked Coral Reiser.

Graham gave her an icy stare. "On page twenty-one the word 'repudiate' appears on line twenty. In the first edition the word is 'reduplicate.' The error was corrected in the second edition." He flipped the pages of the book. "The word 'steadfast' here on page 218 was misspelled as S-T-E-D-F-A-S-T in the first edition." He held the book up toward Coral

Reiser and pointed. She nodded as did several others. "I think it is clear why I think a missing book is stolen."

Everyone was stunned, and the room was quiet until Graham passed the copy of *The Scarlet Letter* over to Mary, who looked through it quickly and passed it on to Bernadine, who took more time with it.

Edmund Linehan bent forward so that he could see the three guests just beyond Dr. Lehr's shoulders and spoke directly to the ladies. "Carlton-Stokes has been noted for its Archival acquisitions for almost one hundred and fifty years. Because the college was founded by an off shoot of the early Christian Disciples and is the oldest institution of higher learning that that sect supports, we have been blessed with all of the church's historical records plus some gifts from extra generous benefactors . This led, very early in our history to acquire not only documents but works of literature and history as well."

"And music," added Coral Reiser.

"And music," agreed Edmund Linehan.

"Actually, Carlton-Stokes wasn't the first of the brotherhood," broke in Onorio or Charlie. "We had a college in Chucktucky as far back as 1836."

"That's true," continued Linehan, "but that school had financial troubles and closed down not many years later. We have all the records of that college in our Archives. (Note that we always use an accent in speaking of our Archives.) We are now, however, the oldest college founded and supported by the brotherhood, as George likes to call The Christian Disciples."

"We are not simply an institution hording valuable artifacts," added George from the other end of the table and looking directly at Dennis Marlin. "Some of the material is merely stored here, but most of it is part of continuing research. Many members of our faculty are here because of our rare collection. Badger makes good use of our literary works. Edmund is something of a national treasure himself. He knows more about the Civil War than any man alive, and Carlton-Stokes is the best place I know in the world to study the war from the Missouri north or the Mississippi west. It certainly isn't his salary that keeps him here. Charlie studies the print styles and bindings, and earlier you heard how Miss Reiser makes use of the Archives for its special music."

Bernadine looked at George and smiled. "And what about you, George? Tell us what special value does a professor of romance languages get from a collection that so favors America?"

"Simple. From my readings in French I became interested in Edgar Allan Poe, as most of the really important criticism of his work is in French, not English. We in America ignored him for years. At C-S I have ample material on Poe to add to my French research on him."

"Can we get on with it!" Craig said in a loud voice. "I don't have a whole lifetime to devote to the history of this little school." He bore the air of pure innocence as if the term "little school," had surely no pejorative intention, or was it an amoral air like unto Hawthorne's Donatello in *The Marble Faun* ? Badger looked under the table to see if Craig had shoes or hooves.

"Yes, I have a number of things to do before I go

to bed," said Marlin.

"'And miles to go before I sleep, / And miles to go before I sleep.'" quoted Badger with Blanche not far behind.

"What was that?" asked Marlin.

"Oh, nothing. We just thought a little Robert Frost might be in order," responded George, trying to rub sand in the oyster.

"Yes, we should get on with it," said Graham. "The problem is much larger than this one book. After the discovery this morning and after calling all of you, I started going through other volumes in our collection and have found one other forgery, and who knows how many more will be found when we make a thorough search. I have here." He stopped talking and rummaged through a stack of papers in front of him then pulled out a sheath of papers. "I have here a list of all the books, manuscripts, and documents in our collection. You should each find a copy in front of you. Sorry ladies," he said to the Badger sisters and Mary, "I didn't think to have any extras run off."

"I'll look on with Dr. Lehr," said Edmund, as he passed his copy over beyond Bernadine to Blanche.

"I have marked all of the missing books with a red check mark. Our first edition copy of Thacher's*History of the Town of Plymouth* has been replaced with a homemade binding over blank pages, and our facsimile copy of Thomas Jefferson's *The Life and Morals of Jesus of Nazareth* is missing outright. Thatcher's book goes back to 1835 and only nine hundred and fifty copies were printed. I couldn't even guess at its value. That isn't my area."

"On the current market, it's worth about three thousand dollars," volunteered James Craig.

Is that all!" said Mary, whose proximity to Graham had made her quite a bit bolder than she might otherwise be. " I would think that if only nine hundred and fifty books were printed over a hundred and fifty some years ago that it wound be worth a great deal more."

"Thatcher was no Shakespeare or even Hawthorne," explained Craig in a condescending tone. "Book value is a matter of supply and demand. Limited copies will raise the price only if their is a demand. Most people, have never heard of James Thatcher, not even most scholars."

Graham decided he had better take back the floor. "I obtained the Jefferson volume myself after searching all over the country for it. Nine thousand copies were authorized by Congress in 1904 for their exclusive use. Fewer than a hundred copies remain today, if my estimate is correct, because of the corrosive chemicals in both the paper and the binding. I was able to find one of the few that had been kept in a protective cover so that it was not exposed to the air. It doesn't have great monetary value because it is just photo copies of Jefferson's single copy."

"I've never heard of such a book," broke in Mary. "I thought that Jefferson only wrote on social and scientific subjects."

Graham may have been upset initially to have had the three women thrust upon him at the beginning of the meeting, but he was now delighted to have an audience of so high a caliber, the Badger sisters sitting prim and proper and Mary Mallony asking all the right questions. "Thomas Jefferson took four translations of passages in the *New Testament* where Christ speaks, and pasted them side by side in a blank volume. He then compared the Greek, Latin, French and English versions. Someone found the book for our Congress around 1890 or so. It was then photocopied, or more properly, a photolithographic process was employed, then the work was bound handsomely in red Morocco and ornamented in gilt. Three thousand copies were printed for the use of the Senate and six thousand for the use of the House." Copies naturally found their way into the hands of the descendants of the congressmen of that time, and as I said before, most are now destroyed. It's value was not in money. It was probably worthless to most of the people who possessed a copy. Its value is to libraries and institutions like ours."

"So, at the present count," said Badger from the other end of the table, "we are missing our first editions of *The Scarlet Letter*, *The People, Yes*, and *History of the Town of Plymouth* and our copy of *The Life and Morals of Jesus of Nazareth*. Anything else?"

"Isn't that enough?" said Graham, "There is one more. One of our two copies of Kate Chopin's *The Awakening*. It's irreplaceable."

Badger wondered if the phrase "in a snit" had been created by someone who knew Graham.

"I should say it would be!" said Bernadine. She is one of the most ignored writers of the last century and one of the best."

"You know her work, then?" said Graham, a bit surprised and a great deal irked that the spotlight had been focused elsewhere.

"Indeed we do," broke in Blanche. "There isn't a girl, now woman, who attended Sacred Heart Convent who didn't know her work. She was an alumnus you know, just as were all of the Badger sisters. The nuns thought her work a bit too scandalous for our young eyes, so we had to find copies elsewhere. The poor girls today can't even find a copy in the public libraries. Your grandmother, Badger, wrote a dramatic skit on what was thought to be one of the more erotic chapters and presented it at an assembly. None of the sisters even blinked. It was scandalous only in its own time."

"It would seem, then, that someone is rather effectively stealing a few of our valuable books. Any idea when this was done?" Badger asked.

"I know the Jefferson book was here last month when I, myself, used it," said Graham. "Both the Thatcher volume and the Chopin could have been taken at any time within the last year or so, but *The Scarlet Letter* was here last week. This I know because I was using it for a paper I am preparing for the *Philology Quarterly*."

This, thought Bernadine, Blanche, Badger and probably a few others, almost in unison, helps to explain how Graham Carruth could be so precise on spellings and page numbers.

"Did someone think to call the police?" asked Coral Reiser, looking directly at Graham. It was quite clear to all present who "someone" was.

"No, Miss Reiser, I did not." Graham directed his attention to Mary and the Badger sisters. "You see, our local police consist of one unqualified, elected town marshal and his incompetent appointed assistant. They are good at checking our few parking meters and fair at being school crossing guards."

"Coral is correct, nevertheless," said Badger. "We had better protect ourselves legally and call Marshall Rutan. It might be a good idea, also, to call in the state police."

Graham just sat in his chair and looked at his list. Coral Reiser pushed her chair back with just enough scraping to draw everyone's attention but not so much that it detracted from her ladylike qualities. "I suppose I can make both phone calls." She walked to the front of the room and paused next to Graham and held out her hand. "I will need the keys to your office to use the phone, unless you want me to use the pay phone down stairs." Graham reluctantly gave her his keys and she left the room.

Again Graham turned to the three women. "All the phones in this building except the one in my office and the pay phones are connected to the switchboard and it is unfortunately closed at this hour and over vacation."

"Who would steal such books?" asked Edmund Linehan. "I should think they would be very difficult to sell. The buyer would certainly want some proof of authenticity."

"Yes, they would," said Gary Jurgenson, breaking his silence. "You couldn't put them on sale at a local book fair or even in a rare book store, but I suppose there are places."

Dennis Marlin let out a volcano of smoke and cleared his throat. "It might be a bit difficult," he said , "but not impossible. I've been in stores where I'm sure there were shady dealings going on." He lit another cigarette. "And the books would be easy to sell anywhere in Europe."

"Someone who did manage it might become very rich in the process," added Onorio Flores. "Some of the books in the Archives are true art treasures. I don't understand why the thief didn't take more books while he was at it."

"That's a very interesting question," said Badger, "and a very interesting choice of books taken. The Scarlet Letter would bring a great deal of money as might The Awakening. The other three would bring very little. Thank you," he said to George when the second edition of The Scarlet Letter was finally passed to him.

"Don't you think it's just possible that the thief took the books for his own collection, you know to keep hidden?" asked Charlie.

"That's right," answered a rather smooth voice belonging to Jack Zinecor. "Any collector would sell his soul for a first edition of The Scarlet Letter."

"Speak for yourself," said James Craig. "I would certainly like to have the book, but I wouldn't do anything dishonest to obtain it. Don't judge everyone by your standards." He tugged on a Vandyke that Badger felt sure was doctored to keep as black as his obviously doctored hair.

"Well, of all the gall!" yelled Zinecor, "and from someone who played such a cheap trick to get that first edition of Capote's *Tree of Night*."

"That book is worth under a hundred dollars," Craig yelled back. "We were talking about *The Scarlet Letter.*

"Gentlemen, gentlemen!" cried Marlin, banging on the table with his fist. "Let's not get into petty little arguments. Let's stay with the problem at hand."

Badger had been sitting back leafing through *The Scarlet Letter* and only half listening to the men argue. "Wouldn't this second edition be almost as rare as the first and have some real monetary value?" he asked to no one in particular."

"Yes and no," said Graham. "The second is nearly as old and nearly as rare as the first, but its value is limited. "Few people are willing to pay a large sum of money for a second edition, although a genuine book lover would certainly treasure it."

"That's true. I have a number of second editions that I treasure said Jurgenson.

"I think, then," continued Graham, "that we can conclude that the thief was interested in keeping the stolen book, and hoping that no one would notice the switch. After all, there would be a little more profit in stealing the book outright and it would be a great deal easier. The Thatcher book also would be a collector's item. With it, also, there was a real attempt to conceal the theft. Why the Jefferson, Sandburg and Chopin books were stolen outright I as yet have no idea, but I intend to find out."

"Did I miss anything?" Coral Reiser walked briskly into the room and sat down, again smiling at George.

"Not a thing, Miss Reiser. Did you get through to the police? It certainly didn't take you very long," said Graham.

"Marshall Rutan is in Quincy, his night off," she explained. "I told his deputy to have the Marshall come up the Hill first thing in the morning."

"What about the state police?" asked Badger.

"I told them to wait until morning, also."

"How could she tell the police what to do?" asked Blanche. Everyone turned and gave her an incredulous look.

"That's good," said Graham. "That way my friends here and I will be able to finish checking the rest of the Archives for any more irregularities before the authorities start poking around into everything. I finished this room by myself."

Badger wanted to say, "Goody for you," but restrained himself. Instead he said, "Well, if that's all, I guess we'll leave so that you can get to work." He got up, as did all of the other members of the faculty along with Bernadine, Blanche, and Mary. They slowly filed out the door, leaving Graham with his four belligerent experts, who sat looking at the table top as if it had just come to life.

"I really hate to leave you," George said, pulling Badger aside, "but Coral wants me to drive her car home for her. She hates driving at night. I'll see you up here in the morning. Give my apologies to the ladies. You have good taste in aunts and in lady friends." He took Coral Reiser's arm and steered her past the other faculty, out the door, down the stairs and out of sight.

"There is one thing that I find rather strange," said Bernadine as they moved towards the others. "It may be spring vacation, but I can't imagine that all of the faculty except those few that were here tonight would be out of town."

"Oh, they aren't. Most of them are in town. Some are even on the Hill. In fact, I saw Alice Pragman and Al Daniels yesterday shortly before you arrived. They're in the English department with me. They simply stay away as much as they can. Most of us assign term papers to be turned in right before vacation. Then we all crawl into our little holes and grade papers for a week. I knew you were coming so I stayed up late nights to finish mine by Thursday."

The four joined the remaining faculty, standing by one of the tables and Onorio Flores tried to entertain the Badger sisters and Mary with various slight of lip tricks: "I am pleased that you like my name," he said. "I also appreciate beautiful names. Mary is a name most sacred in my religion and Bernadine and Blanche. These are such unusual names and so alliterative. Why were you named so?"

"It was our mother," said Blanche. "She was a very alliterative person. She had nine children."

CHAPTER IV

LATE HOLY THURSDAY NIGHT

Alive, this man was Manes the slave: but dead,
He is the peer of Dareios, that great King.
                        "Epitaph of a Slave," Anyte

"What do all of you think about Graham's problems?" Badger asked his guests once he had them settled back in his apartment on the second floor of the Victor and Eva Gibson home on Fifth St. in Walden.

The four had returned to the flat after saying good-bye to the three faculty members, had all "used the facilities" as the Badger sisters always said, and had taken the same places in the living room they had had earlier that evening. Badger had sliced generous helpings of chocolate cake that Eva Gibson had baked that morning for her favorite (and only) tenant. He had boiled water for instant coffee, his great accomplishment as a chef, poured it, and set snifters of brandy before the three as well as one in front of his own chair.

"Very strange, and not a little problem at all," said Bernadine. "As I understand it from what was said tonight, only the college staff members have regular access to the Archives, and I find it hard to believe that any one of the faculty we met tonight would steal the books."

"Of course," said Blanche, "We have only met a few people. We can't assume that just because someone has an education that he is honest. Don't forget Bradley Wilbur." Blanche was referring to the lawyer who had murdered Mary Mallony's husband just a few months before when Badger spent his Christmas vacation with his aunts in Oak Meadow, Illinois, had solved the crime and found a new interest in the person of Mary.

"I agree with Blanche," said Mary, "but emotionally I feel just as Bernadine does."

"At this point," said Badger as he lit his aunts' cigarettes then his own, "I am much more interested in the crime itself than in who committed it. "Why would any sane person go to the expense and the considerable trouble of forging a first edition, faking a cover on another, and then simply stealing three additional books from the shelves? The methods here are varied. It's almost as if more than one person were involved, and that hardly seems likely."

"What about a break in?" asked Blanche. "Maybe someone forged the two books and substituted them and then someone else broke into the library and stole the other two. Two unrelated crimes. That would explain the various methods."

"I know that things like that happen and perhaps that happened here, but I doubt it. I'm not a Thomas Hardy; I just can't accept 'hap' or coincidence the way he did," said Badger.

"How about a prank?" suggested Mary. "On a college campus that is always a possibility. Some students can be very resourceful."

Blanche flicked the ashes of her cigarette into the ash tray and sat back on the couch. "Remember, Bernadine, the time I came home from the library and told you how a group of high school students checked out all of the 800 poetry books? They said they did it so the shelves in that section could all be dusted." She turned her head to Mary. "That was when we used the Dewey Decimal System, before we switched to the Library of Congress."

"Yes," agreed Bernadine. "Every year a group of boys from an academy near one of my libraries would steal an old bust of Longfellow in the entry way - on Longfellow's birthday. They found some very interesting places to hide it."

"I think our students know the difference between a prank and the theft of a valuable piece of property. Besides, they would have no reason or method for the elaborate forgery. Where would they obtain a second edition of *The Scarlet Letter*? No, there has to be some other explanation. I guess we'll have to wait until morning to see if any other books are missing. And if there are, the problem becomes more serious, but it might be easier to discover a pattern. No one but Mary has tried the cake. I assure you Mrs. Gibson is an excellent cook and an even better baker. Chocolate cake and brandy go together."

"It would seem that we have been of no help in this matter," said Bernadine.

"On the contrary," said Badger. "You have all been a great deal of help. You have suggested possible solutions. I'll keep them all in mind and mention them to the state police in the morning. You have also given me a chance to think out loud. That's always a help."

The four dug into and finished their cake and coffee while discussing the college and the town of Walden at the same time enjoying their snifters of brandy. It was past eleven o'clock when Badger heard Mrs. Gibson calling his name from the bottom of the stairwell.

"Badger! Phone call!"

Badger excused himself and went out the door and down the stairs as fast as he could manage on his short legs. Mrs. Gibson in high heals, tight slacks, and loose blouse was waiting at the foot of the stairs, running her fingers through her silver hair.

"I'm sorry, Eva. There must be an emergency. No one ever calls me after 9:30."

"It's perfectly all right, Badger. It didn't disturb me. I was just watching some t.v. and waiting for Vic to get home."

Badger went into the Gibson's apartment, through the living room to the kitchen where he picked up the receiver hanging down from the old fashioned wall phone.

"Badger Smith."

"Badger, this is Graham. I thought it best to call you tonight rather than wait until morning. That will give your deductive mind a chance to sleep on some new facts. There are some additional missing books, four altogether. We've found a forged *Wieland*, you know, the Charles Brockden Brown novel, and a forged copy of *The Spy*, Cooper's book. Then we found that some books were just plain missing. That Robinson book you and George picked up for me last year is gone, and a really strange one, *The Hill* is missing!" Badger wasn't sure, but Graham sounded almost jubilant, not the way he had earlier in the evening and not the way a curator should when some of his most valuable property has been stolen.

"That is strange, Graham, and it does give me something to sleep on. Is there anything else?"

"No. My four helpers went home, as I am doing. They'll be up later in the morning. I just thought I should tell someone and you seemed the logical choice. See you in the morning." He didn't wait for a good night but hung up."

Badger replaced the receiver and walked back through the living room where Eva Gibson was watching a commercial for dog food and chewing on a granola bar.

"Your guests like my cake?"

"They loved it, Eva. Thank you. It topped off the evening."

"Any time."

"Thanks again. You say Victor's coming home tonight?"

"Supposed to. Called me from Louisville last night and said he'd drop off his rig in Quincy somewhere around eleven and be home here around twelve tonight."

"Well, I'll see him then tomorrow. I've got a few things to talk over with him."

The commercial had changed to one for blue jeans so Eva didn't hear Badger's last remark. He closed the door quietly and climbed back up the stairs and entered his apartment. The three women had stopped talking the second they heard him and were waiting expectantly when he entered.

"A bizarre turn of events," he said as he came in. "Graham and his strange assortment of experts have finished their search and have come up with two more forgeries and with two more books that are missing outright."

"That makes four of one and five of the other," said Blanche. "What are the new books?"

"The two forged books are logical choices, Brockden Brown's *Wieland* and Cooper's *The Spy.*"

"I don't think I know who Brown is," said Mary.

"Charles Brockden Brown. He isn't widely read today," said Bernadine, "but he's quite important. Most consider him the first truly professional American novelist."

"*Wieland* was published in 1798, so you see it predates the Hawthorne and even the Cooper by quite a bit." Badger realized that he sounded like he did in class. "The book was not only valuable, but Graham was slowly photo-copying it because any edition of it is hard to find."

"Why slowly copying?" asked Bernadine.

"Because he didn't wish to damage the binding when he held back the pages and he didn't want to subject the pages to too much heat at one time and discolor them."

"Yes, now what about the missing books?" asked Blanche.

"Very, very strange. One was Edwin Arlington Robinson's *Matthias at the Door* and the other was Wade Watts' *The Hill*. Last Year when George and I took a trip to New York, Graham asked us to pick up *Matthias* for him because he knew there was a copy available. It's signed and numbered. We were able to get it at a good price, just over two hundred dollars. I would guess it is worth anywhere from two hundred dollars to four fifty. A drug addict might steal something worth that but not someone who can make forgeries and takes truly valuable books."

"What about *The Hill* ?" Bernadine asked. "I don't think I've ever heard of it or the author."

"And you shouldn't have," said Badger. Wade Watts was one of the faculty members of Carlton-Stokes about twenty years back. *The Hill* is an attempt at a history of the college. Everyone here has always called the campus "the Hill." The College Board of Directors was so pleased with Watts' scholarship and all the pictures, and maps and blueprints that he dug up that they saw to it that the book was published. It is a truly beautiful volume with leather tooled binding and slick paper, all gold leafed. It's written in the fashion of a scholar and gentleman and is, as a result, almost totally unreadable. In a garage sale you might get as much as a dollar and a half for it." Badger looked around the room for reaction.

"These are very strange books to steal!" said Blanche. "Who would take the risk of stealing a book worth only a few hundred dollars . . . or one that you could get little more than a dollar for?"

"Someone who wanted the book for himself and couldn't get it any other way might steal it," answered Badger, lighting a cigarette and washing down the smoke with a bit of brandy. "On the surface that seems to make sense with the Robinson book, since there were, if I recall, only five hundred copies numbered and signed by the author and that was in 1931, I think. Many of those books would have been destroyed by now, making it a difficult book to find." He took a hard pull on his cigarette and let some of the smoke out his nose and the rest escaped his mouth as he talked. "However, anyone who had the wherewithal to take a second edition of Hawthorne to help forge a first edition would certainly be able to obtain a copy of *Matthias at the Door.*"

"Of course there is one other possibility," said Mary. "It could be that the thief didn't know the value of what he stole."

Badger thought this one over. "You may be right, Mary, but I don't know how that fits in with the forgeries."

"We just keep going back to the idea of two different thieves, and two seperate thefts don't we?" said Blanche.

"Yes, and I still find something strange with that idea, unless, of course, the forgeries represent books that were stolen and the rest are just misplaced or lost over the years," said Bernadine.

"The only problem with that is that Graham is far too careful and meticulous to allow such a thing," said Badger.

"I don't know about you young girls," Bernadine said, looking at Mary and Blanche, "but when you get to be my age, beauty sleep is not only for Beauty, it's also for the Beast." She rose slowly from the couch.

"True," said Blanche. "We really should be getting back to our quarters." She and Mary also stood up after finishing their brandy.

Badger crushed out his cigarette and rose, almost knocking over a lamp in the process. "I'll show you all back to the Student Union."

"That's not necessary," said Mary. "We can find it without any trouble. Besides, if you drove up with us you would have to walk back down the Hill."

"In this lovely weather that really isn't much of a chore. It gives me a chance to think."

"But it's late at night," objected Blanche. "There are stories in the newspapers every day about people like you being mugged or stabbed or beaten!"

"You're in Walden, Missouri, not New York or Chicago. This is almost as peaceful as Thoreau's Walden. Fraternity initiation night is about as wild as this town ever gets and our fraternities are tame," He held the door open for the three as they gathered their purses and left Badger's apartment, Bernadine in a slow lead with Blanche and Mary close behind.

CHAPTER V

HOLY THURSDAY INTO FRIDAY

*In the Spring a livelier iris changes on the
burnished dove;
In the Spring a young man's fancy lightly
turns to thoughts of love.*
        "Locksley Hall," Alfred Lord Tennyson

The ride up the Hill was as quiet as is possible in a year old Lincoln that has never had its oil changed. Badger directed and Mary turned whatever way he said. By this time, however, she needed no direction, as Walden and the campus of Carlton-Stokes were simple acres to maneuver.

When they pulled up in the lot next to the union there wasn't a soul about. Badger escorted the three into the building and up to the desk where a gangling young man of about twenty was half sleeping and half reading *Antony and Cleopatra*. He handed Badger both keys. Bernadine and Blanche gave Badger and Mary each a kiss, agreed to meet for breakfast at eight o'clock in the Lion's Den, took their key and went quickly to their room. Mary held back.

"I hate to go to bed on such a beautiful night even if it is late. Did you notice all the stars as we drove up?"

" 'Two things fill the mind with ever new and increasing wonder and awe - the starry heavens above me and the moral law within me.' "

"Is that yours?"

"I'm afraid I can't claim it. It's Emanuel Kant's, or the person who translated him into English." He took her by the hand and led her out the door, where the stars burned their beauty into the night. Once outside it seemed natural to continue to walk on the cement path that led to the now dark Carl Bach Library about six hundred yards ahead of them.

"You couldn't have planned a better day than the one we have had," Mary told him. "For starters, the cocktails and the dinner were delicious."

"The dinner was all George's doing. I cook about as well as I sew and I'm sure you noticed the missing button on this shirt."

"George is a delight. He added immensely to your party. And the diversion! Bernadine and Blanche are in their glory with this mystery of the missing books. It's almost as if you had planned it like one of those 'How to Host a Murder' games in the stores."

"What about you? Are you enjoying it?" Badger asked her.

She squeezed Badger's hand and pulled him to a halt. "Once I married William my life pretty much came to an end. After he was...after he died, my life slowly started to come back. Now, standing with you on this beautiful night I'm not ashamed to say I feel like a school girl again, and you, John Badger Smith, are the cause of it." She stood close to him and kissed his lips then turned and began walking too quickly for Badger to do more than walk with her. They strolled on for a time in the happy silence of lovers.

"This is a beautiful campus. I wish we could stay to see it when all of the students are here."

"I thought you were going to stay! I so wanted you to sit in on some of my classes. The students start returning Sunday and they're all back by Monday night. Tuesday in my poetry class we're doing T. S. Eliot's 'The Waste Land.' I was counting on your being here. If you're not, then April will truly be the cruelest month."

She squeezed his hand. "We'll see," was all she said.

Beyond and just to the left of one of the men's dormitories they could see the lights of Walden below them, and just beyond it the moving lights of a river barge heading toward St. Louis. The sky was a reflection of the earth, each star twinkling like a lamp below.

"There's no husbandry in heaven," said Badger, to himself.

"What's that?" asked Mary.

"Oh, just a bit from *Macbeth*: 'There's husbandry in heaven; Their candles are all out.'" They walked on, wondering at the stars until they had stepped off the path onto the parking lot Mary had first pulled into that afternoon."

"There's husbandry on campus, too; their lights

are also out," said Mary, as they looked at the dark buildings.

"Not exactly," said Badger. "Look behind the Library. See the way that one tree trunk sparkles? There's a light in one of the rooms at the back, reflecting on the tree. Stay here and let me check." Badger let go of Mary's hand and did a slow canter to the rear of the library, stopped, looked about and returned to where Mary stood waiting.

"One of the windows in the Archives is all lit up. Graham must still be there. Let's see if the door is unlocked. Maybe he has a bit of further news."

They walked briskly to the front door, but it failed to open when Badger pulled.

"Do you suppose if you knock?"

"No one would hear, not even if I banged. There are a number of doors between here and the Archives. We might try the one on the loading platform."

They walked around the building, not bothering to go back to the sidewalk but stepping through the grass and following the bushes that outlined the library. They reached the back and began climbing the stairs to the loading platform. Badger stopped on the top step.

"Wait a minute. If Graham were here we would have seen his car in the lot, and the lot's empty. I've a funny feeling in my stomach."

Mary pulled up beside him. "Maybe it's just the janitor cleaning up."

"I don't think so. The janitor would have had very little to do since most of the offices have been empty all week and the library itself has only been used by a few students. I would guess that someone simply forgot to turn off the light."

Badger stepped to the entrance way and pulled on the handle of one of the two panels. This time the door opened. He held it for Mary with one hand while fishing in his pocket for his cigarette lighter with the other. The hallway they entered was small and dark. The lighter barely gave enough illumination for him to find the wall switch and flick it. The warm darkness was replaced with a cold and almost frightening light. The floor, walls, and ceiling were all concrete and the single light bulb hanging from a cord above them sent shafts of illumination that resembled a drawing of the sun by a first grader. A single door in front of them was tried and found wanting. It wouldn't budge. They pushed open the double swinging doors to their right and stepped through to the stairway beyond. Badger found another switch and flicked it. A light on the second floor shown down on them with the same cold intensity as the bulb in the hallway. Badger again took Mary's hand as they started up the steps. The concrete not only bounced the light; it did the same with the sound. Their footsteps sent the message of their coming up the stairwell and probably far beyond. Something told them not to speak.

At the top of the stairs stood another door, like a medieval dragon guarding a secret treasure. It was, however, a flameless dragon, as it opened noiselessly at Badger's first pull. They found themselves in a narrow hallway that led to one of the library stacks in one direction and to a door directly in front of them. They could see the light bleeding out of the crack between the floor and the bottom of the panel. Badger turned the nob and pulled. It was locked. He banged on the door but there was no response. He banged again.

"Is anyone in there? Open up!"

"Don't you have a master key?" Mary asked.

"That shows how little you know about academia," said Badger. "The great truth of all pedagogic institutions is that keys are doled, and I do mean doled, out to anyone who is hired part time or full time to sweep floors, but no teacher is ever deemed trustworthy enough to carry more than the key to his own office, which he can't reach unless a janitor has unlocked the outside door. Graham is, of course, one of the very few exceptions."

Badger stooped down and put his eye to the keyhole. After a minute he stood up quickly. "I think there's someone lying on the floor in there." He took out his wallet and extracted a credit card. "I saw someone do this in a movie once." He dropped to his knees and slipped the card in the crack by the lock. "That must have been a Charlie Chaplin film. Let's see if we can go out through the library and down to the public phone on the first floor."

The two walked down the narrow hallway into the library, with Badger flicking every light switch he saw on the way so that there was enough illumination to guide them to the circulation desk and the main switch box behind it. He flipped a switch and was rewarded with instant noon. The double doors to the stairway had a lock on the inside so they had no trouble getting to the first floor and the phone. Badger reached in his pocket and came up with three pennies and his car keys.

"You have any change, Mary?"

Mary fumbled in her purse then dumped out the contents on an isolated conference table against the far wall. As she was scraping through her belongings the two heard a bang behind them, some scratching sounds and then the door opening that led to the passage to the hall they had first entered off the loading dock. This happened all too quickly for them to react in any defensive way.

"What's goin' on here?"

The two turned to face a short, wiry man in blue jeans and a blue and white Carlton-Stokes letter jacket with a big C-S on the pocket.

"Doug Boito! You're just the one I was trying to call."

"Oh, it's you, Prof. Smith! Saw all the lights flickin' on as I was comin' up the Hill. Came up to check on one of my men. What's goin' on?"

"Doug Boito, this is Mary Mallony one of my guests this week-end. Mary, this is Doug Boito, the superintendent of buildings and grounds." Doug Boito and Mary both nodded their heads and looked embarrassed. "We were walking on campus a little while ago and saw a light from one of the Archives' windows. The back door was open and we investigated. The door was locked but through the keyhole I saw what appeared to be a body on the floor." As Badger said the words he realized how silly they sounded.

"Let's look." Doug was a man of few words in the simplest of times, and in times like these he was terse. He led the way back up the stairs, through the double doors and down the narrow hallway to the entrance. The ring of keys hooked to his belt every day of the week, even in church on Sunday, made an almost Christmasy sound on this Holy Thursday. He unhooked the ring, selected a key, slipped it in the lock and turned it. The door, which had been poorly hung years before swung open without any help and the three stood facing an overturned bookcase, scattered books and papers and the body of a man, a man who looked to be very much dead.

Doug Boito and Badger stepped into the room, leaving Mary standing in the open doorway looking at the body. It was lying face down on the floor. A large bloody gash on the top of the head told them that this man was definitely dead. A doctor could have told very little more.

"We better not touch the body," Badger warned Doug Boito. "Can you tell from the back who it might be?"

"Larry Sermons, night man. Guess he came in to goof off an' knocked over that bookcase." Doug Boito stood up.

"You're right! It does look like Larry Sermons. Glad you could recognize one of your own men."

Doug shuddered. "Hardly one of my own men. Sermons was hired a couple years ago while I was in the hospital. Been trying to get rid of him ever since. Does as little as possible then sits all day in Aunt Kate's, swilling that bile she calls coffee, complainin' 'bout how hard he works at night. "He's the one I came up here to check on. I'll go call the marshal an' state police." This last he said over his shoulder as he left the room.

Badger remained quiet until Doug's footsteps no longer sounded down the hall. "Doug Boito is a good man. The students love him. The football team made him an honorary letterman. I don't think he's had that jacket off since. All the faculty consider him one of us and not simply staff; however he's not quite a police detective. I'm not sure I would accept his conclusion."

Mary stepped into the room, not to be closer to the dead man or even Badger but to be out of the cold light of the hall and into the fluorescent glow of the Archives. Having faced her own husband's murdered body not many months before, Mary was not afraid of a corpse, but was troubled that death seemed to be pursuing her.

Badger moved carefully about the room examining everything in sight but touching nothing. He found a few books with a bit of blood on them, a paper cup on the table with cigarette butts floating in the remaining coffee, and a number of scratches and gouges in the table and chairs. Since the bookcase was turned over on its face he realized that he would have to wait until after the police had righted it in order to examine the front. The other bookcases that lined the wall seemed to Badger to be untouched by whatever had happened here. He stooped down and using the credit card he had placed in his pocket but had not returned to his wallet, flipped over the pages of the book lying closest to the corpse. It was an autographed copy of Badger's own slim volume of verse, with the title almost every poet ultimately uses, *Poems*. "No loss here," he said and stood up. "But I wonder why it would have been close enough to the corpse to have blood on it. Unless Graham has a new type of filing system this book should be over there in that bookcase." He pointed across the room.

The clicking of footsteps sounded down the hall and a moment later Doug Boito reentered the room. "Called Rutan an' state police. Both on their way. Prof. Carruth wasn't home."

"As soon as they get here," said Badger, "I'll ask to let you go back to the union. Nothing more will happen tonight that you won't learn about in the morning. You look tired. And you did come down here for a vacation, not a police investigation."

"You think it's more than an accident, don't you, Badger?"

"I just can't stand so much coincidence, forgeries and thefts in the Archives and now a dead body. I'm sure it's murder."

CHAPTER VI

GOOD FRIDAY MORNING

Oh, give us pleasure in the flowers today;
And give us not to think so far away.
                    "A Prayer in Spring,"   Robert Frost

Badger woke as his clock radio clicked on and a female voice from the Quincy station announced that it was six-fifteen, the weather partly cloudy with a chance of rain in the afternoon, and a high near seventy-two. He pulled himself from his bed and stumbled to the bathroom, leaving the door open so that he could hear the news when he wasn't running the water. It wasn't worth hearing about: A car bombing in Crete, a minor earthquake in California, a new health care plan proposed by two western congressmen, the Mississippi rising above the Keokuk dam, and a three car accident on Route 24 east of Quincy, then a long segment on all of the nearby minor league baseball team loses. Nothing at all about the death of Larry Sermons.

Badger completed his ablutions, including a shower performed on his knees with a hose attachment that looked like a rusty piece of conduit, then dressed himself in gray slacks, blue and white sport shirt and a blue sport coat he should have given away years ago, turned off the radio, crossed the hall to his living room and kitchen, and poured himself some orange juice while he leaned against the sink and then ate an uninspired breakfast of soggy corn flakes with extra sugar and milk and went over the events of the previous day.

Graham Carruth found several valuable first editions had been replaced by forgeries and several other books were missing outright. Mary, Doug Boito, and he had found Larry Sermons dead in the Archives amid a turned over bookcase and scattered books. When he returned to the library after seeing Mary back to the union he found that Wash Rutan, the town marshal of Walden, had passed the entire episode off as a few misplaced books and an accidental death when Sermons had escaped to the Archives for a little coffee and a smoke. A detective sergeant from the Missouri State Police named Reburg was inclined to think that there was more to the death than bumping a bookcase too hard, but he was not inclined to explain why. The raised bookcase revealed nothing more than a number of fresh gouges and scratches. The body had been removed to the local mortuary where an autopsy was to be performed this morning by Dr. Peacock and the Walden undertaker, Ronald Drial, who was also the county coroner, president of the Walden Chamber of Commerce, president of the local school board, and secretary- treasurer of the Methodist church.

Badger rinsed out his glass and cereal bowl and left them in the sink. He was halfway down the stairs when he realized that he was going up the Hill to have breakfast with Mary and his aunts and had just filled up his stomach with the tasteless generic corn flakes he always purchased in order to save money.

The air was crisp and clean, just the way he liked it, so he was quick to make up his mind to walk. The weather man might see rain in the clouds, but Badger saw only romance in the sky. The early morning sun cast long shadows from the trees around him.

Taking the route that led past the Catholic church at the foot of the Hill he began climbing the steep wooden stairs that would take him to the student union building. He was well winded when he reached the top and turned to look back down the Hill. He could see a man in a black cassock. Father McLaughlin was opening up the front door of the church below him. Even the steeple was lower than the campus Hill. The blue and brown Mississippi flowed in the distance outlined by the green of Illinois just beyond. When Badger looked up, a cloud in the shape of a crocodile seemed close enough to reach out and touch although it was thousands of feet above him.

"Quite a sight, isn't it."

Badger whirled around to see Sgt. Reburg sitting on a bench, partially hidden by a huckleberry bush that had only a few days before full bloom. He was dressed as he had been the night before, in brown slacks and blue sport coat with a nondescript tie adorning a white shirt. He looked to Badger like the secret service men he had seen on a trip to Washington a few years before, except that Reburg was older.

"Somebody sure picked a great place to plant a college. If the school weren't here I'll bet our legislature would turn this into a state park and the whole place would be filled with beer and pop cans and hamburger wrappers." He stood up and stepped over to the walk to meet Badger. If one could somewhere find an aesthetic crow and fly him over the two men, he would be sure to see a likeness to Asher Brown Durand's *Kindred Spirits*.

"What's your subject, Professor?"

"English, mainly American literature."

"Yes, that's right. The way you were looking at the sky I thought you were ready to break out with a bit of Robert Frost."

Badger laughed. "Not only English majors admire the sky. Some of my students, who are decidedly not interested in English or any other academic subject that I can imagine, spend a great deal of time with their heads in the clouds."

"Care to give me your reasons for believing Larry Sermons was murdered?" Sgt. Reburg was not one to waste a great deal of time on niceties, Badger realized.

"I don't believe that I said anything to you last night about murder." Badger was slightly taken aback.

"No, but I suspect that you would take the opposite view of anything Marshal Rutan would say. Besides, your facial expressions gave you away."

"I see. You're correct, of course. I do believe he was murdered. First, I don't like the coincidence of the missing books and then the corpse. That alone would be enough for me; however there is more, and I suspect you saw the same things I did. If Sermons had bumped against the bookcase and knocked it over and been killed then the case would have been on top of him or at least part of him. Second, the wound on the head was right on top. If the bookcase had hit him it seems to me the wound would have been to the side or to the back of the head, not right on top. It's not hard to believe Sermons was involved in thebook thefts somehow, knowing his reputation. "

They had started walking slowly toward the union, each with his hands thrust deep into his pockets. "Those scratches on the furniture suggest rather strongly to me that the bookcase hit the tables and moved them to where they were when we came in."

"True, and what is important about that?"

"The paper coffee cup with the cigarette butts in it was sitting undisturbed on the table, and it couldn't have been there when the bookcase fell or it would have been knocked to the floor. Someone had to have placed it there afterwards, logically the murderer."

"I thought maybe you had noticed that. That's why I waited for you on the bench this morning where I could see you walking up the steps or parking in the lot over there. I knew you'd be coming up to see your aunts and lady friend. Yes, I made a few inquiries about you and yes, I already knew you taught American literature, wrote poetry, and had some interest in rare books. You see, Professor, I can handle the murder investigation, even the references to literature, and I can call in all kinds of experts from district headquarters, but the Sovereign State of Missouri has no experts on rare literary volumes to send out. I need someone who knows something about books and a great deal about the workings of this college and who has a good enough eye and mind to see the importance of the paper coffee cup. I would like you to work with me."

"Anything I can do I will, but I'm hardly an expert on rare books," Badger assured the sergeant. "Anything in particular you want me to do?" They had reached the entrance to the union and stood there rather than enter.

"There is to be a meeting at eleven o'clock this morning of everyone who attended yesterday's meeting, as well as your astute town marshal and yours truly. I would like you to use your temporary authority as your president's representative to chair the meeting and steer it in the direction I indicate, first by going over in great detail everything that has happened. I've found that people tend to be a little more themselves if I remain in the background. I'm hoping we will get the results of the autopsy before too long. That might help a bit. But for now, I'd better get back to work. I've got a crew of men, and a few women, checking on everything, and doing God knows what, including interviewing students." He turned and started toward the library without saying good-bye but simply waving his hand.

Badger entered the student union, read a bulletin posted on a tag board then walked into the Lion's Den. Bernadine and Blanche were seated in a booth, side by side, facing him, each with a mug of coffee in front of her that steamed enough to tell Badger that they hadn't been waiting long. They both wore flowered print dresses and spring hats of yellow straw. Blanche waved her hand and Badger smiled, waved back, stepped over to them, and slid into the booth and faced them.

"Where's Mary?"

"That is a fine way to greet your two great aunts on a gorgeous Good Friday morning," said Blanche, giving Badger a coquettish smile. "I think that you should start over."

"I wonder how our new friend Onorio would enjoy that bit of alliteration, Blanche?" said Bernadine.

"I'm sorry. Good morning, Bernadine. And good morning, Blanche." Badger got up and came over to their side and kissed each of his aunts as she turned her cheek to him. He returned to his side.

"Good morning, Johnny. Mary took a shower so is taking a little while to get her hair dry," Bernadine informed him.

An attractive coed placed a mug of coffee in front of Badger. "Ready to order, Prof. Smith?"

"We'll wait a bit, Jessica. We have a fourth joining us."

"Are you really working with the police on the murder of that janitor, Professor?"

"Yes, I am, Jessica, but I really can't talk about it now. Maybe I'll have some information of interest by Tuesday during our nine o'clock class."

Jessica nodded and went back to the counter, giving everyone a parting smile.

Bernadine looked at the table. "How could we have ordered? There isn't a menu here or anywhere else that I can tell."

Badger pointed in the direction of Jessica. "The menu is on the wall behind the counter. Difficult for you to see without craning your neck. I can read it to you." He knew that Bernadine could not read what was printed on the board at that distance no matter how much neck craning she did. Her poor eyesight, like her arthritis, was something no one was supposed to mention or even notice.

"We can wait until Mary gets here. In the meantime perhaps you could fill us in on your gallivanting last night after you put Blanche and me to bed. Mary just gave us the briefest of details this morning."

Badger blew over the cup then took a sip of the black coffee before giving his two aunts an account of the happenings of the night before, of course, leaving out the kiss and hand holding; although his aunts probably added them mentally. "The state police sergeant and I are sure that the death wasn't accidental. I'm sure somebody deliberately struck Larry Sermons. We have a murder on our hands." Both Bernadine and Blanche smiled noticeably. Violent death was a terrible thing, but if someone *had* to be murdered wasn't it nice that it was done close by so they could be involved in the investigation? Of course, they would say prayers for the repose of the soul of Larry Sermons' in church on Easter Sunday, but in the mean time, reading murder mysteries, as they both did, was a great pleasure, but actually being embroiled was much, much better.

"This looks like a happy group." Mary Mallony slid into the booth and sat next to Badger. Like Bernadine and Blanche, she wore a flowered dress and a hat, blue rather than yellow. However, her hat was more of a sun bonnet so that she had to turn her head all the way to the right in order to see Badger. "Have you ordered breakfast yet?" The attractive coed moved from behind the counter and placed a mug of coffee in front of Mary then proceeded to refill the other mugs from a carafe she held in her left hand. In the Lion's Den there was one drink in the morning, coffee, and there was only one way to drink it, regular, strong and black, except for those few, but then there are always a few of those wherever one goes.

"If they have fried eggs I'll take one sunny side up, with orange juice, small," said Bernadine.

"Make that two," said Blanche.

"That sounds good to me," said Mary.

"Make it four, Jessica," said Badger, but I'll have two eggs and ham on the side. And I'll take a large grapefruit juice instead of orange."

"Ham on Friday, and Good Friday at that!" exclaimed Bernadine.

"Right. Forget the ham, but bring me some toast."

"You had better bring us all some toast," said Bernadine.

Jessica smiled again at them. "Back in a sec." She returned to the counter where she spoke into the serving slot to an unseen short order cook.

At that moment Badger remembered the corn flakes earlier that morning. It didn't matter at all, he told himself. He had exercised both his body and brain since leaving his apartment. He was in need of further nourishment. He sipped his coffee.

The conversation was one of catching Mary up

on the events since she left the library the night before. All conversation stopped except for "Thank you," when Jessica returned with all four of the breakfasts stacked up her left arm. She had trouble finding any place to put the plates of toast as the booth was small and the plates large. Once she left and the egg yolks had all been ceremoniously broken, Blanche took a sip of coffee and looked apprehensively at Badger.

"Since there is murder involved now, shouldn"t you get hold of the president of Carlton-Stokes so he can be in charge?"

"That would be wonderful, if I could, but Jonathan Hayes, our president, is somewhere in Georgia or Alabama on the chicken ala king circuit raising money for the college, and because his secretary is on vacation no one knows exactly where that somewhere is, and even if I could contact him there is nothing he could do about all this. Besides, if President Hayes were here you might not be invited to participate in our little mystery." He gave Blanche a quick smile. "I think now that the state police have been brought into it we will move along quickly. It is not at all like having Marshal Wash Rutan in charge." Badger opened a small carton of raspberry jam and spread some of it on a half piece of toast. "Oh, by the way, Sgt. Reburg wants us all in the room at eleven this morning for an update."

All three women wore large smiles that went well with their spring hats. The four finished their breakfasts in relative silence, contemplating the investigation. Jessica made several more trips to their table with her carafe of coffee and coquettish smile.

"When this mess is all through I think I'll write

a parody on "Gunga Din" using Jessica as a coffee bearer: Though they curse and then berate you ,/ (Pronounced berade) / By the livin' Gawd that made you,/ You make a first rate cup of coffee, Little Jess.

Two male students who had been sitting in a rear booth got up and walked toward the door, passing Badger.

"Good morning, Mr. Smith," they said in unison.

"Good morning, Scott and Jason." responded Badger.

"Mister!" exclaimed Blanche when the two boys had left the Lion's Den. "What happened to 'Professor' or "Doctor'?"

"In small colleges the students and faculty are too close for formalities. I call some of my students by their first names, if I can remember them, and they call me Mr. Smith, and a few call me Badger."

"What about our waitress, she . . . ," started Bernadine.

"Jessica is a very nice young lady working for A's in all her classes. She needs them for architectural school next fall."

Bernadine insisted on paying the check when the four had finished eating their eggs and toast and drinking their juice and all the coffee that Jessica had been able to carry to their booth.

Outside, they strolled along the walk that Mary

and Badger had used the night before. Instead of stars, this morning they had large billowing clouds that caught the sun's pewter rays and turned them to silver. Instead of the lights of Walden they had the spring greens and yellows mixed with the blue of the Old Man. The campus itself was as lovely as ever, but it lacked the usual parade of students from one building to another. Only a few were in sight and they were hardly on parade. State police were more abundant than scholars, talking with the few students available, measuring this and that, and searching through the bushes around the library building. Five police cars were parked in the lot, making the library area look just like a state police headquarters.

The four stopped in front of a large girls' dormitory which stood above the library and to its left and which offered perhaps the best visage of the Mississippi. They had well over a half hour to enjoy the spring day before going inside to the meeting.

"The one place on Campus where you get a better view is from my classroom over there. That's because it's on the second floor."

"I see you're showing the girls the sights of the campus." George came upon them by way of an intersecting walk that wound around the dormitory. "Good morning, all. I assume you are taking your time getting to the meeting."

Everyone greeted George, who, ignoring the welcome, continued talking. "Graham called me earlier and gave me his second hand account of the adventures of our own Robin Hood here and his maid Marion. I'm anxious to hear it from the horse's mouth, if you don't mind a mixed metaphor this early on a spring day, but I suppose I should wait until you fill us all in at the meeting." Mary was smiling but Badger was decidedly blushing.

"I think that someone is waving to us," said Blanche, pointing toward the library entrance, where a female figure was flapping both arms at the group and then beckoning with her left hand.

"That's Coral," said George. "She seems to want us to hurry over, and I don't see any reason that we should antagonize such a lovely lady on such a lovely spring day."

The five began walking rapidly toward Coral, as rapidly as Bernadine could manage with her arthritis and emphysema. George went ahead at a half gallop followed by Mary and Blanche. Badger walked beside Bernadine, and talked the whole time about the great importance of walking slowly after eating breakfast. By the time they were all in front of the library George had been properly briefed.

"Everyone is here and set to go, They want us to start early," George told them, then took Coral's arm and lead the group inside.

"Interesting that all are so anxious to get started," said Badger as he and Bernadine again fell behind. "Natural curiosity or what?"

CHAPTER VII

GOOD FRIDAY MID-DAY

But tell us no more
Enchantments, Cleo. History has given
And taken away; murders become memories.
"To Cleo, Muse of History," Howard Nemerov

All of the assorted committee members, book experts, and police were in place in the Archives room, and Dr. John Badger Smith was seated at the head of the table or, from Graham Carruth's vantage, the foot. This did not look like people about to delve into the events of robbery, forgery, and murder, thought Badger. It looked to him more like spectators waiting for the kick off of a championship game. The seating arrangement from the night before was modified as follows:

Wash Rutan

Badger Smith

Karl Lehr	Mary Mallony
Bernadine	Onorio Flores
Blanche	George Mercater
Ed Linehan	Coral Reiser
James Craig	Jack Zinecor
Gary Jurgenson	Dennis Marlin
	Doug Boito

Graham Carruth

Sgt. Reburg

Wash Rutan had taken up a position in a straight chair in front of the door that led out into the library. He had the chair tilted back and his feet on the rung. Sgt. Reburg stood leaning against the door that led to the interior rooms of the Archives. He was in position to catch Badger's eye very easily without being noticed by others.

After a period of forty-five minutes all the details of the forgeries and thefts had been recapitulated with the same force as the four note motif in Beethoven's *Fifth*. And the death of Larry Sermons had been explained to everyone. Sgt. Reburg kept his mouth closed, even when Marshall Wash Rutan called Sermons' death accidental. When Badger started to mention the coffee cup, Sgt. Reburg caught his eye and shook his head, and Badger let it appear that accidental death was the official view.

A hard rapping at the library door almost knocked Marshall Rutan from his perch, but he somehow managed to right himself, swing the chair out of the way and open the door. A uniformed state policeman spotted Reburg and called across the room. "Wanted on the phone, Sarg, the coroner."

The room remained silent the first few minutes Reburg was gone. But then Coral Reiser turned to George and asked with her usual smile. "Have you invited them yet?"

"Invited who? What?"

"You know, George, about the *Creation*.

George looked across the table at Bernadine and Blanche. "Coral here is leading a chorus and orchestra of Walden folks in a performance of Haydn's *Creation* Sunday evening at the Church of Redemption, and she would very much like all of you to attend." He twisted his head around Onorio Flores to include Mary. "We naturally assume Badger will join the group."

"We're not going to do the entire oratorio," explained Coral. "You see, we are limited both in voices and instruments since most of the students are gone, but it should be an interesting evening of good music. Dr. Lehr was good enough to allow us to use his fine church."

"We would love to come," said Bernadine. "Johnny, why is it you aren't singing with the group? You have a beautiful voice." His aunts thought him gifted in everything.

"Or why aren't you playing in the orchestra?" Blanche chimed in. You are a very talented bass violinist." This she said even though she had never heard Badger play.

Sgt. Reburg came back into the room, whispered into Badger's ear, then walked around the table and stood just behind Graham Carruth.

"The phone call was from Ronald Drial, the coroner. He and Dr. Peacock have just finished the autopsy." He was playing this announcement like a ham actor in community theatre. He waited until he was certain several people were ready to scream. "They have concluded that Larry Sermons died after cracking his skull. A bit of skull fragment pierced his brain. They said that he was dead before he even hit the ground." After another pause he continued.

"He was struck with some kind of blunt instrument, hard. Larry Sermons was . . . . . murdered."

In the B movies of the nineteen thirties that Bernadine and Blanche used to watch on a big screen mid-week in a movie theater and that Badger watched any time he could on his small screen t.v., that announcement would have been followed by such a confusion of sound as to make the little gathering at the tower of Babel seem a polite conversation in braille. In this instance, however, no one spoke. Everyone but Badger and Graham Carruth glued his eyes on Sgt. Reburg and waited. Badger and the sergeant looked around the room to catch any unusual reaction. After a silence strong enough to fill a black hole, Coral Reiser raised her right hand like a school girl. Sgt. Reburg acknowledged her with a nod.

"Why would anyone want to, ah, do that to Larry Sermons?" Somehow she couldn't bring herself to use the word "murder" or even "kill."

"A very good question," responded Reburg, who like so many who have been quizzed, used the four word complementary preamble to collect his thoughts. "A very good question, indeed. There are a number of possible answers to it, but it is too early in our investigation to give the definitive one."

"Well, perhaps you could give us some of the possible ones," pressed Coral, not to be put off by anyone.

"Yes, like Coral, I, too, would like to hear some answers," said Dr. Lehr. If Larry Sermons was murdered, as you say, then many people will want answers: town folks, trustees, faculty, and parents."

Several others gave affirmative grunts or nodded their heads.

"Perhaps it would be a good idea if we came up with as many conjectures as possible," said Badger "This might prompt a few other possibilities from the group."

"All right," said Reburg. "Since he was struck as he was we can assume that his assailant knew him. They were in the room together. Robbery seems a very unlikely motive."

"He might have been carryin' somethin' on him that was taken," said Wash Rutan from the other end of the room.

"He *might* have, but robbery is still unlikely. The violence of the act and the force used suggests it was done by someone who was either extremely angry or one who wanted Sermons dead. As likely as not, the killer had not planned a homicide. Sermons was too large a man for someone to plan to kill in such a way."

"Or by someone hoping it would appear unpremeditated," said Edmund Linehan.

"There is no doubt that the theft and forgeries of books certainly had something to do with it," continued Reburg.

"Couldn't they just be coincidences?" asked Onorio Flores. "There is a great deal of difference between stealing books even valuable books, and murdering a man."

"That is true," admitted Badger, "But there are

just too many coincidences for me to swallow. Books missing from the Archives, and other books missing and forgeries left in their place, also in the Archives, and then a man is killed, murdered, again *in the Archives*. These crimes are all connected. Of that I'm certain."

"The missing books could very well just be misplaced," said James Craig. When there are so many people who have access to these rooms it's easy to see how a few books could be mislaid."

Jack Zinecor lifted his eyes slowly off of the pencil he had been studying intently. "We've checked every book in the Archives , Jim, and found nothing. Don't you remember?"

James Craig noticeably colored when he was addressed in such a casual fashion. "I remember distinctly. I also remember that we didn't look through the general library at all. The missing books could very well be there."

"The search of the library has already begun, but it will take a good deal of time and more manpower than we presently have," said Graham. "Even if all the books were found that wouldn't explain the forgeries."

"Those forgeries, as you call them, might be what the Archives had all along as the real thing. You know," said Gary Jurgenson, you are not always the most methodical of men. Last year you allowed over a hundred books to slip by without being properly checked out, I read it in the school newspaper."

"And what about all of those books found every June in empty dorm rooms?" asked Coral Reiser.

"I think you will find that Graham Carruth's record on lost and stolen books is much better than that found on other campuses," put in Edmund Linehan. "Suppose we get on with the proceedings."

Both Badger and Sgt. Reburg would have been happier to let the little donnybrook continue, as so much can be learned by just letting people talk. After all, thought Badger, listening to students express their views and evaluating them in class was not really very different from listening to these people around the table.

"Thank you, Edmund," said Badger. "As I was saying, there is just too much coincidence to overlook it. I think we have most of the information we need to figure out something about the missing books, and if we can make sense of it, perhaps we can solve the murder as well."

"What information do we have on the missing books aside from what they were?" asked Bernadine.

"I think that Graham should answer that if I may ask him a few questions," said Badger. "Graham, tell us what was the physical appearance of Wade Watt's book, *The Hill,* say as opposed to the other missing books."

"It was truly beautiful. Remember the books published by the Heritage Club starting in the late forties? Well, *The Hill* looked like that. When Doctor Watts had the college agree to pay for the printing of his history of the college he worked directly with the printer, a St. Louis firm best known for doing art reproductions, to get the best paper available, the finest cover, the best ink. He even had some of the photographs tinted. And there was extensive art work."

"In other words, the book was one that would highly impress anyone who had no knowledge of its contents."

"That is true. Oh, yes and the cover was hand tooled."

"I don't understand the loss," said Bernadine. "Surely if the college paid for its publication there must be other copies around campus."

"There are," said Graham. "Boxes and boxes of them. They are stored in Woodruff Hall. We just haven't had a chance to bring another copy up to the Archives. When we do, I'll have a number of copies sent so that you can all have one."

"You have already stated that *The People, Yes* is a handsome volume, which is true also of Jefferson's *Life and Morals of Jesus of Nazareth,* " said Badger. "I can certainly attest to the attractiveness of Robinson's *Matthias at the Door,* since I helped to obtain it for the Archives."

"I believe that I get your point," said Edmund Linehan. "All of the missing books that were without forgeries in their places were extremely attractive and would lead any novice to believe they were books of great value."

"What about Kate Chopin's book?" asked Blanche. "I'm sure that that would be just an ordinary volume with nothing much to excite anyone to steal it unless he knew its contents."

"An interesting thing about that book," said Graham. Several months ago I noticed that the lower spine on *The Awakening* was unraveling. Not unusual for a book that is referred to as often as that one. I repaired the book as best I could then temporarily placed a dust cover over it. I forgot about it and never got around to taking the dust cover off. The thing is . . . . . the dust cover was a sheet of very strong, gold Christmas wrapping paper. I had written the title across the spine with a silver marker, making an extremely attractive book, if I do say so."

"The other books all had substitute volumes in their places," said Badger. "Albeit not all the substitutes were forged with the same care. So, attractive books, mostly of limited monetary value, were stolen outright while worn, old volumes of great value were forged. I'd like to jump to another topic for now. What can any of you tell me about Larry Sermons? Dr. Lehr?"

Dr. Lehr was occupying himself with a fly who, like all flies, had burgled in by an outer window, then stolen in though the door and alighted on the table in front of him. He tried with his two index fingers to snatch up the drousy spring habinger but was just a mite too slow. Badger found himself comparing Dr. Lehr with young Tom Sawyer and the pinch-bug. The Archives was no church and Dr. Lehr no Tom Sawyer, but somehow they fit together in this Mississippi River town. The doctor leaned forward on a plain wooden cane today. The fly wearied of the game of tag and flew off to buzz above Onorio.

"Very little. I knew who he was, and would say hello to him if we passed in town or when I was on campus. He usually responded with a grunt or a nod. He never was in my church - or any church I know of.

I really don't believe he knew who I was."

Badger looked past Dr. Lehr. "Bernadine and Blanche, of course, didn't know him. How about you, Edmund?"

"I was actually on reasonably friendly terms with Larry. He was unquestionably the laziest janitor on any campus, but early on in his sojourn with us I found a way to get him to do things for me. He knew who I was because my name was on my office door and he was assigned the cleaning of most of the offices in this building. One day I found myself short of Xerox paper and didn't have time to requisition more. I poked my head out the door and said, 'Larry, I don't suppose you have the authority to get some Xerox paper from the storeroom.' His pride was at stake. He said he certainly had the authority, and he got me the paper. I used that phrase with him many times and it always worked. 'I don't suppose you have the authority.' One other thing. Larry helped me one time. He came in my office one day when I was on my hands and knees looking for a rather special old fountain pen. My folks had given it to me when I graduated from high school, before the days of the more fashionable gold watches. I had kept it in perfect condition and had it sitting on my desk as an ornament. It must have rolled off. I told Larry about it and he found it in a corner. I gave him a reward, I remember."

"How much?" asked Reburg.

"Ten dollars, I believe."

Badger turned his head and looked straight down the table. "What about you, Graham? What can you tell us about Sermons.?"

"Never got along with him. Found him more than once in this very room and several others, with his feet up on the furniture taking an extra long break with coffee and a cigarette." He looked over at Dennis Marlin.

Badger looked at the group and smiled. "My own experience with Larry was interesting. I would often leave the library at closing time and find him at the foot of the stairs by the door, sweeping, so that everyone leaving the library would see him supposedly working. He loved to ask me, 'Read any good books lately?' Then he would laugh. My point is, he wanted people to think he worked hard, when he didn't, and his idea of humor left no doubt with me that he hadn't read a book in many years, if ever at all."

"I don't think we should speak ill of the dead," said Coral. "I didn't know this Mr. Sermons other than to recognize his face. He was always around to close up the auditorium after a concert."

"An interesting bit of information," said Doug Boito, speaking for the first time. "Larry Sermons was never assigned to Blendhiem Auditorium. At the time your concerts let out he should have been either here or in one of the lecture halls, depending on the night, but never in the auditorium."

"But I would see him all through the concert," Coral continued. "It used to bother me a great deal that he was always in the wings close to the sopranos during the performances."

"I should say I never hired Sermons," said Boito. "That took place while I was in the hospital. Someone in the business office took him on and Jim

Giester was too soft hearted to let me fire him. I've had a first class crew except for Sermons."

"I think, that tells us a great deal about Larry Sermons," said Badger. "All we need for now, at any rate. Did any of you gentlemen know Sermons?" Badger looked to each of the experts.

A cacophony of sound followed. "When would I ever see one of your janitors?" "Never get up here at night." "May have seen him, but don't recall." "Definitely not!" These responses were given so quickly and close together that it was difficult or maybe impossible to tell who said what. Badger noted how the four resembled the three monkeys plus one: See some evil, hear some evil, speak some evil, and think some evil. They had three things in common: a great knowledge of rare books, gigantic egos, and very carefully controlled jealousies of Graham Carruth. Why?

Sgt. Reburg caught Badger's eye. Badger understood. "Well, I think we can draw this meeting to a close. It is getting on into the lunch hour. Perhaps, Graham, we should schedule another meeting for tomorrow sometime, if it is convenient or maybe even if it isn't. We might have something more to go on." Sgt. Reburg gave Badger a smile and had one returned.

"We five are planning to start checking the general library this afternoon, with the help of some students and any of you who would like to assist." He looked around the room as all heads looked down except those of Bernadine, Blanche, and Mary. "We will be here tomorrow as well. If there are no objections why don't we all meet here about one o'clock Saturday afternoon." This was not a question, nor was any objection anticipated nor time allotted for one.

Graham Carruth stood and everyone followed his lead. The room emptied out rapidly except for Mary and the Badger sisters. Badger stepped out with Sgt. Reburg at his side, just behind George, who was enjoying the task of helping Miss Coral Reiser into a light colored, spring jacket that contrasted becomingly with her dark hair.

"I think, Prof. Smith, that we have learned a great deal from this short meeting. I would like to compare notes with you. I'd be happy to treat you and your lovely guests to lunch at Aunt Kate's Diner, if Aunt Kate's lunches can be considered a treat. It will be your aunts one chance to ride in a police car."

"We would love to, provided you drop the Prof. Smith and call me Badger, the way everyone else does."

"Agreed, Badger, provided you call me Chuck."

The Kindred Spirits waited for the ladies to join them then walked at Bernadine's speed out of the library, down the steps and over to the parking lot where Chuck Reburg's police car waited next to several others. The women filled the back seat comfortably, but were cut off from the men in front by a wire reinforced window partition. The sergeant indulged himself and the ladies by blowing the siren all the way down the Hill, through town to the highway and Aunt Kate's, where they pulled into the only parking space available.

"It would seen that the entire town of Walden comes to Aunt Kate's each and every noon time to indulge themselves in some of the culinary world's most unusual delights," the sergeant said as he opened the rear door and helped the ladies out, as the entire town, or what had sardined itself into Aunt Kate's strained its collective neck to get a look at the group as the siren wound down and stopped.

Aunt Kate, herself, opened the front door and ushered the five to a table at the far end of the restaurant. She scraped an extra chair along the floor from another table and motioned for the group to sit.

Aunt Kate, whose name wasn't Kate , who had no brothers or sisters, and who had no friends younger than sixty and those were all female with busts considerably smaller than Kate's own formidable brisket, had one attribute: a business with the best location in all of Walden.

The five seated themselves, read through the menu, ordered, and waited for Kate's other patrons to weary of their celebrity status. Hearing a police siren in Walden and then seeing Aunt Kate escort someone to a table are "such stuff as dreams are made on."

Aunt Kate returned with one ham on rye and four cheese sandwiches, french fries, and various drinks: coffee for Mary and Chuck, tea for Bernadine and Blanche, and milk for Badger.

"Aunt Kate, what can you tell us about Larry Sermons?" asked Badger. Chuck Reburg was remaining just as silent in town as he had been in the Archives. "We understand he came in here almost every day of the week."

Kate motioned to her only waitress, a high

school girl with a yellow apron that had at one time been white, to fill the water glasses, waited for the task to be completed, looked each of the five in the eye, then spoke directly to Badger, ignoring the others as if they weren't at the table. "I ain't one to speak against the dead, you understand, Prof. Smith. An' I believe in mindin' my own business. Live an' let live or die is my motto, but that Sermons character was somethin' else. He come in here every mornin' 'bout eleven an' plops hisself down at the counter, orders coffee, with double cream, mind you. Then he starts gabbin' 'bout how hard he works up on the Hill an' how Doug Boito is a slave driver. If I'm busy an' not watchin' him, he swipes a doughnut or two from off the covered tray. Worst customer I got, or had. God rest his soul."

"Did he ever do anything worse than steal doughnuts, that you know of?"

"Just taking double cream was bad enough. But he'd try sellin' stuff in here to anyone he thought would buy it. I think he stole it, if ya ask me."

"What kind of *stuff* did he try to sell?" Badger tried to hold Aunt Kate, who looked as if she were about to go after her waitress.

"Always little personal stuff, stuff that looked like it come off someone's desk up at the college. You know, paper weights, letter openers, pens, that sort of stuff. An' he musta done pretty good with his thievery in the last week or so."

"What makes you say that, Aunt Kate?" asked Blanche. "Did you see people buying things?" Blanche took healthy pleasure in pronouncing the words 'Aunt Kate.'

"Oh, once in awhile I'd see someone slip him a buck or two for somethin,' but that's not what I meant." Aunt Kate had actually looked at Blanche as she answered the question. "Last week or so Larry been actin' awful high an' mighty an' flashin' a fat wallet. Even told Mike Alft over there that he'd pay for a big night on the town in Quincy. Not sure, but I think I heard him say something about driving over in his new car."

Chuck Reburg slipped out of his chair and strolled over to where Mike Alft was sitting at the counter entertaining several of the locals .

"Did he ever try to sell any books to anyone here?" Bernadine was now being the sleuth hound.

"If you knew Larry you wouldn't ask a question like that, Honey. Larry Sermons never read a book in his life, lessin it was porno an' someone read him the five letter words." This last she said over her shoulder as she moved away from the table. A big smile was meant to complement herself on her great wit.

"I think we have all the reinforcement we need on the character of Mr. Larry Sermons," said Chuck Reburg slipping back into his chair. "Mike Alft over there says that Sermons bought a used Chevy over at Berry and Jack's gas station down the highway. I'd say he was certainly involved with the book thefts. All we have to do now is figure out how he was involved, and prove it, then show how it all related to his murder."

"That should be an easy task," said Blanche, who noted that even state policemen were somehow not as bright as her Johnny.

❦   ❦   ❦

CHAPTER VIII

GOOD FRIDAY NOON!

it is a strange day a strange day
even the arichoke has disappeared
                    "silent day," John Knoepfle

𝕱ew   things in this world could   keep Badger
Smith quiet when he wanted to talk, but one of them was
lying prone before him, one of Aunt Kate's infamous
cheese sandwiches, with pickle on the side. The
bread was always a bit stale, the crust hard, but the
cheese warm and melted, sticking to the teeth in such
a way that speech,   if not difficult was at least
embarrassing.   Coffee and tea helped to clear the
problem,   but milk seemed to compound the difficulty.
Badger was the last of the group able to communicate.
The other four had passed beyond the niceties of the
occasion, the strangeness of the the day, and were
ready for a further recititive on the character of Larry
Sermons before Badger was able to join in the
gossip.

     "Since I am paying for this sumptuous repast,"
said Chuck Reburg, looking at Badger, "I think I am
entitled to your thoughts on Larry Sermons and his
involvement in this case."

     Badger used his tongue as best he could to
clear Aunt Kate's lunch from the front of his teeth,
finished his milk, and began in a voice far too loud for

his intention. "Larry Sermons was a lazy and ignorant thief," his voice softened, "known to almost everyone in this community, including, I believe, our four experts who tried to act as if they had little or no aquaintance with him. He was contacted by someone to substitute the forgeries for valuable books for which he received some small sum."

"That all seems like what we know of the man, Johnny, but what makes you say it?" asked Bernadine. "What proof do you have?"

"Well," began Badger, who now had clean enough teeth to continue, "Everyone attests to his laziness, including Edmund, who got along with him. The fountain pen incident and what Aunt Kate said suggest rather strongly that he was a penny ante thief. That he was murdered in the Archives after a series of book thefts of various types says, at least to me, that he was involved. He is certainly one who would take a book like *The Hill* thinking it was worth money and leave behind the truly valuable books that the Archives is crammed with. Sermons was down here almost every day, and at one time or another, almost everyone in Walden and most of the county enters the hallowed halls of Aunt Kate's. I'm sure his murderer saw and heard him here and contacted him to do a little extra-curricular work. My guess is that the murderer paid Sermons outright for his services, thus the money Aunt Kate saw him flashing around.

Mary broke in. "You keep talking about the murder and the murderer, Badger, but when you and I and Doug Boito found the body it was in a locked room. Don't you remember?"

"I do indeed. But it was a spring lock. Philo

Vance mysteries have complex solutions which I greatly admire, but most puzzles have simple solutions."

"Just as there was with the locked room when William was murdered this past Christmas." Bernadine was referring to the murder of William Mallony, Mary's husband, just a few months before, a reference she knew would not bother Mary.

Badger continued as if no one had spoken. "And I'm sure there is a simple solution here. Wash Rutan would undoubtedly see us taking this simple accidental death and changing it into a murder, ignoring what the coroner found. I don't believe that the book shelves could ever have inflicted the wound that killed Sermons. They wouldn't have hit him on the top of the head. Someone hit him a blow that not only knocked him down but killed him as well. Then that someone pulled over the book case, making it appear an accidental death and foolishly placing Sermons' coffee cup on the table."

The high school girl came up with a caraff of coffee in one hand and one of hot water in the other. Receiving the proper nods from Mary and Chuck she poured coffee. "We didn't have a chance to see the murder scene as you and the sergeant did. Could you describe it for us," said Blanche. "That would help a great deal."

Chuck Reburg was reluctant to describe the bloody view to two elderly matrons, but Badger held no such compunctions. "Just think of the final scene in *Hamlet*, but with only one body."

"Where Fortinbras says, 'Such a sight as this / Becomes the field, but here shows much amiss,'" said

Mary, beating Bernadine and Blanche by a fraction of a second.

Badger's already soft heart melted a few more degrees. The way to some men's hearts may be through the stomach, as Fanny Fern attests, but the way to John Badger Smith's heart was through Shakespeare. "That's the spot, Mary. When the bookcase was righted Sermons lay there. The floor was covered with blood and littered with books. Graham and his four helpers are going to have a very difficult time cleaning the blood off those volumes."

"Was the blood on the top or underside of the books?" asked Bernadine.

"On the underside except for a few. I see you get the point."

Everyone looked at the smiling Bernadine. "If the books had fallen from the bookcase when it killed Mr. Sermons then most of the books would have landed *before* blood could have been splattered, meaning the books would have been bloody *on the top* not on the underside. The way it happened shows that the body had fallen and bled, before the books, and naturally the bookcase. I rest my case, books and all."

"That's correct, Miss Badger," said an impressed Sgt. Reburg. "Your nephew and I had determined that someone struck Sermons and then knocked the bookcase over on top of him, as Badger said earlier."

"Neither Blanche nor I ever allow potential beaux to buy us lunch unless we are on a first name basis," said Bernadine. "You are a potential beau, are you not?"

"Indeed I am, Bernadine!" said Chuck.

"What about the blunt instrument?" asked Mary. "If, as Badger said earlier, Larry Sermons was struck by someone who had not come there to kill him, then the weapon should have remained in the room and it would have been there when Badger and Doug Boito and I got into the room."

"Murderers often take the weapon with them to complicate the investigation, which it certainly has in this case." Chuck Reburg was looking down at the check that Aunt Kate had just laid before him. He looked around the table. "Is there anything else I can order for you? More coffee? Dessert?" All heads shook. "Well then, I guess we should be going."

Once outside, the five piled into the police car once again and prepared for another ride, this time up the Hill. Badger again took the seat next to the sergeant and said something to him as be buckled his seat belt. Chuck Reburg put the car in gear and pulled out onto the highway, but instead of turning to drive up the Hill he continued on straight up the road several blocks to where a large sign announced a Marathon service station. He pulled up to where a man was putting air in a tire. Badger opened his window.

"Hi, Rog."

Rog looked at the police car then at Badger. "Finally caught up with you, huh, Badger?"

Rog, these are my aunts from Oak Meadow, Illinois, that I've told you about, and a friend, Mary Mallony. Bernadine and Blanche, this is Roger, the best mechanic in the state."

"Pleased to meet you all. I know your nephew here has been anxious to have you come down to Walden for a visit. Hope you're enjoying yourselves."

"Rog, what do you know about that Chevy that Larry Sermons bought here last week?" asked Chuck Reburg, stepping out of the car and walking around to where Rog was now standing.

"Hi, Sarg. Sounds like you need a little work done on your brakes the way they just squeeked. That Chevy was an '89 Capris with low milage. Belonged to Patty Clark over in Kahoka. She kept it in real good shape. We just parked it over there with a sign on it an' Sermons bought it the next day."

"Happen to know what Sermons paid for it?"

"No, but Jack and Berry know. Jack's on a call. Berry's in there."

Reburg nodded and went inside. The four could see him talking to Berry in the office beyond the glass door.

"You all workin' with Sgt. Reburg on Sermons' death?"

"Something like that, Rog. Was Sermons a regular customer here?"

"Not very likely. If he ever bought gas it was from someone else and he never changed his oil. He left a cloud of smoke bigger than the Lone Ranger. He just saw Ms Clark's car settin' over there where we always put cars for sale. Don't know what he did with His old car wouldn't run no more. "

Reburg slipped back behind the wheel. And slammed his door.

"Thanks, Rog. Berry put me down for first thing Monday to check on the brakes. You going to do the job?"

"No. Both Berry and Jack are better brake men. Tell 'em I said so when you bring the car in."

They spun out onto the highway and turned to the left to go back up the Hill. Badger waited a few moments, posing his question.

"Mind telling me what Berry had to say about the car sale?"

"He walks in one morning last week and wants to know how much for the Chevy. Far as Berry could tell Sermons hadn't even looked over the car. He sure as hell hadn't looked inside or under the hood because Berry had the keys hanging on a hook in the office. Anyway, he gave him the price, and Sermons pulls a wad out of his pocket and plunks down the dough. Cash he gives him!" When Berry asked him where he got the dough Sermons gets snotty and says it's none of his business, but then he says his grandmother died and left him some money."

"Even Wash Rutan ought to see Sermons guilt now. What was that business about taking your car in for a brake job? Don't the state police have their own garage.?"

"Sure, they have several dozen over the state; unfortunately none of them is anywhere near here. So I take the car in for routine work right here in Walden.

My car gets good service, Berry bills the state, and the state saves money. Also helps me to know the locals."

The library building was caught in a glow of sunlight as Chuck Reburg pulled his squad into the parking lot. The police cars were still in there and uniformed officers were still moving in and out of the building. "I've got some work to do before I let all these men get back to their usual tasks. I'll be in touch, Prof. . . .I mean, Badger, and I look forward to seeing you ladies again." He nodded to the ladies and was gone.

"It would have been better if Chuck had let us off at Lueker Hall so you could freshen up or take a nap or something," said Badger.

"Take a nap! John Badger Smith, what do you think we are, old ladies?" said Bernadine. I would like to use the facilities, as I'm sure we all would, then find a nice comfortable conference room in the library and iron out all we know about the thefts, forgeries, and murder. I believe that Mary and Blanche and I have a few bits of information to help in solving this mystery."

Badger took Bernadine's arm and began walking to the library. Mary followed the example and took Blanche's arm. Both Mary and Badger could feel an increase in gait as they neared the library. Was it imagination or were strains of Harold Arlen music in the air?

Inside the building there was a great deal of activity. A number of students were moving down the stairs to the lower level, called a basement in most places, and bumping into state police at almost every step. A notice on a small bulletin board told why:

MOVIE TODAY AT TWO O'CLOCK
ALEC GUINNESS in
KIND HEARTS AND CORONETS
SPONSORED BY THE INTER- FRATERNITY COUNCIL
50 cents

Badger smiled first at the sign and then at his aunts and Mary. "Usually there are movies only on Sunday afternoons in the projection room, but all this week there have been films. Good ones, too. Nothing after 1950 unless Brittish. Tuesday it was *The Horse's Mouth,* also with Guinness. On Wednesday I checked the library. Every single Joyce Cary book had been checked out. And there aren't many students here right now. So the movies do some good."

The ladies used the facilities on one side of the first floor hall and Badger used the ones on the other side. Then the four climbed the stairs to the library and there found an empty conference room. Actually, all the conference rooms were empty.

All looked to Bernadine as the oldest to begin. "A few valuable books were taken from your Archives and replaced with forgeries. These were discovered quite by accident along with some books that were missing outright, books of far less value but of much greater eye appeal. Please interupt or interject at any time. The two very different methods suggests two different thieves and Johnny doesn't like the idea of two unrelated thieves, nor do I. With the death of Larry Sermons I think much of the problem is cleared up."

"Yes, Johnny, tell us what Sgt. Reburg told you about the car Larry Sermons bought at the service station," said Blanche.

Badger proceeded to tell the three women what Chuck Reburg had told him that Berry had told him that Larry Sermons had said.

"I doubt that your hearsay statements would have much value in a court of law, Johnny, but they certainly present circumstantially that Sermons was involved," continued Bernadine. I would suggest the following scenario: Someone wanted a first edition of*The Scarlet Letter* and wanted it badly enough to sacrifice a second edition in order to obtain it. This person knew that there was a first edition in the Archives and hired Larry Sermons to steal it for him and replace it with the doctored second edition.

"That all makes sense, Bernadine" said Mary, "except we all saw the doctored book when Mr. Carruth passed it around and we could all see the differences he mentioned."

"When someone points out almost anything to you doesn't it seem quite obvious?" asked Blanche. "If Mr. Carruth hadn't pointed out the differences to us we would all have thought it a first edition, including me, and I had a first edition in my care for two weeks."

"I suppose that you're right, Blanche," said Mary, "but there is something very suspicious about Mr. Carruth finding the forged book in the first place, and, if you are right, recognizing it as forged."

"Mary has a point there. I've been wondering about that one myself," said Badger. "But I think we should let it go until later - but not forget it. Bernadine, why don't you continue."

"Larry Sermons did just as he was told - and paid

to do. Having had great success in getting the book he wanted, this person, whoever he was, decided to get another book, *The History of the Town of Plymouth.* He had no second edition to doctor so he bought one of those blank page books sold in every gift shop and printed on the binding. He must have felt rather sure of himself by this time to try passing off such a poor and obvious forgery."

"Don't forget," broke in Mary, "he also forged *The Spy.*"

"And *Wieland,* added Blanche.

"Yes, I forgot. *Wieland* and *The Spy.* Sermons had access to the Archives, so it was he who did the substituting, and, this is my important point, Larry Sermons stole outright the other books. He knew that the books that he had made substitutions for were valuable because our Mr. X had paid him to steal them, so he thought why not steal some other books? And he did. Since he knew nothing of the value of any books he took those that appeared to be valuable." Bernadine stopped and looked around at the three.

"I agree with you, Bernadine. Everything you say makes sense and fits into what we know. But I think we know a few more things than what has been expressed by any of us. We know, for example, that Mr. X, as you call him, knew something about the Archives. He had to know that *The Scarlet Letter,* and *The History of the Town of Plymouth,* as well as *Wieland* and *The Spy* were all there. This he could have learned from talking to Graham, but it is more likely that he had been in the Archives, and more than once. We do know that Sermons spent many a late night hour reposing there, but we now know enough about him to question that he could find those four books on his own. to understand where any particular books were. Mr. X had to tell Larry where in the Archives he could find those particular books. The others he just looked for handsome covers"

"I believe I will accept that idea, Johnny. What else? You said a few. That is plural. You gave us one. What else do we know?" Bernadine had learned years ago that the way to get the best out of Badger was to *badger* him when quizzing her grandnephew on his homework or catechism after his mother had died.

"We know that Mr. X has an interest in rare books that goes far beyond reading them and reading about them. Considering the situation I think we have to say that he is one of the people at the meetings."

"There were women at both the meetings, too, Johnny," said Blanche. Shouldn't we, in all fairness say Mr. or Mrs. X?"

"Are we to include ourselves as suspects?" asked Mary.

"My most facetious friends and relatives, you are not suspects nor is Wash Rutan or Chuck Reburg, but all the rest are - including Coral, George, and me. Personally, I think I am innocent, but all book lovers, especially those with access to the Archives, are suspect and thus suspects. But I think we can eliminate Doug Boito."

"I'm sorry, Johnny," said Blanche. "Me too," added Mary, but the smiles on those two angelic faces showed that they were not in the least sorry for interjecting a bit of their own kind of fun..

Badger smiled in spite of himself. Murder should always be taken seriously but not too seriously, and the subject of murder was what Badger now wished to discuss. " If we are at all correct in the matter of the substituted books and the stolen ones, I think we can assume that Mr. or Mrs. X murdered Larry Sermons. It seems only reasonable that Mr. X was . . . . .

"Or Mrs. X," said Blanche.

"Or Mrs. X, or Ms if we want to be generic," continued Badger, "met with Sermons in the Archives. He would naturally have been angry that Sermons stole those books, especially *The People, Yes,* which exposed the whole scheme, which very well might not have been uncovered or discovered for years, if at all. An argument led to a murder. Murder in the Archives."

"If Mr., Mrs., or Ms X paid Larry Sermons a large sum of money to substitute the books then Mr. X is probably wealthy; ergo Mr. X is not one of the Carlton-Stokes staff; ergo Mr. X is one of the four experts; ergo Mr. X is a mister." Blanche smiled at Badger.

"Very possibly," said Badger, "but I don't think Chuck Reburg would eliminate the others yet and I don't think that we should either."

"In that case , Badger," said Mary, "I think you should tell us something about each of the faculty members. We really don't know very much about any of them."

"Let's see, what can I tell you? Dr. Lehr has a doctor of divinity degree and studies the various church histories in America. That's why he's on the committee. He's been pastor of his church as far back as I know, collects books but nothing of any real value. I know little of his private life except that someone said he has been courting a local widow. He, himself, is a widower, I believe."

"Someone knowledgable in religions of early America would find special interest in all four of the forged books," said Bernadine.

"How do you see that, Bernadine?" said Blanche. *The Scarlet Letter,* granted, with its treatment of mores in Puritan America. The book on the history of Plymouth is obvious. But *Wieland* and *The Spy* ?"

"I'm surprised at you, Blanche. Don't you recall that in *Wieland* Theodore hears a voice that tells him to kill his family and he thinks it is the voice of God, shades of Abraham and Isaac. That certainly fits in with early superstition in America. *The Spy* is not truly religious, but it certainly is moralistic and is Cooper's best historical novel."

Badger sat back, admiring not only his great aunt's knowledge but her quick wit as well. He had not seen the connection of the four books until Bernadine had pointed it out. He wondered, however, if there were any validity to the religious connection. Would a truly religious person steal books to improve his knowledge of a subject? He decided not to ask that question aloud, at least not at the present.

"Back to the faculty. Edmund Linehan has his Ph. D. from the State University of Iowa but got his degree before I was there. He has many hours in literature as well as history. Loves to read fiction and talk about it with anyone interested. Like so many here he has a large collection of books but none of any value that I know of. Married with grown children. One daughter married, another a nun, I believe."

"I don't understand," said Blanche. "There is so much beautiful religious diversity here at Carlton-Stokes."

"That is the real power of this school. There is no prejudice of any kind. Graham Carruth has at least two master of arts degrees, one in English lit. and one in library science. His doctorate is in English lit. I don't know what schools specifically. He has picked up hours from almost everywhere. I think you all have a pretty good idea of his character under stress. Most of the time, however, he is a nice enough person and a top flight librarian."

"Bernadine and I have noticed how well his library operates."

"Onorio Flores has a masters in graphic arts from Illinois over at Urbana. People here call him Charlie, but don't ask me why. He teaches a few classes, but he spends the bulk of his time directing the layout of the school paper, yearbook, catalogue, alumni bulletin, creative writing magazine, and anything else President Hayes thinks up. His wife is an officer in the Walden State Bank. He has a fantastic curiosity so his reading tends to be non-fiction."

"He is also something of a comedian," put in Bernadine. "He seems to want to make us laugh all the time, maybe to keep us from thinking of the crimes?"

"George you know well enough so I'll just say he has his B.A., M. A. and Ph. D. from Michigan. As he said to us yesterday, he has a great interest in Poe, whose works he has in just a few large volumes. You know, *The Collected Works of* . Other than that, most of his books are in French, Spanish, German, or Latin."

"I really wouldn't call George a prime suspect," said Mary.

"Nor would I," agreed Blanche, "but I suppose we had better keep open minds. What about his lady love, Badger?"

"I would be cautious in joining Coral and George. In the few years I've known George he has had a number of girl friends. He fawns over them until they become too demanding then he drops them. Too fond of bachelorhood, I suspect."

"Yes, I believe everyone noticed his obsequious behavior last night in driving Miss Reiser home after the meeting," said Bernadine; "nevertheless what can you tell us about her?"

"Coral did her undergrad work at MacMurray College in Illinois. It is a small school, like we are, so she fit right in from the start. She has her masters from some place in northern Illinois. I don't think she is interested in getting a doctorate. She is not the regular choir or vocal director. Her background is theory and history, but she loves to conduct whenever she can."

"My, don't we have myriad history buffs involved in this situation!" said Blanche.

"She's taken over the choir while Les Pierce is on sabbatical. She's a good teacher and students love her, which, I'm sure you know, does not always follow." I don't believe she's a heavy reader outside of biographies of composers. I've never been in her apartment so I don't know about her library. That's about it. Any questions."

"I have a question, but it's not about the faculty. It's about those four men," Said Mary.

"Fine. What is it?"

"The four men that Mr. Carruth brought in. I understand why you and others find, Marlin and Craig is it?" Badger nodded. "Marlin and Craig unpleasant, but you always group the four and call them 'the experts' in a derogatory tone. The other two I found rather nice, and didn't one of them publish your book?

"What you say is true, Mary, as far as it goes. Jurgenson and Zinecor appear to be nice, quiet men, but I wonder what they are doing here in the first place. Not as a favor to Graham. Jurgenson has told me several times that he thinks Graham a whimpering fool. He calls him 'Graham Crackers all soaking in milk, and soggy. He's here for whatever good it can do him to be near the Archives. He is too much a business man to give of his time freely."

"What about your poems? Didn't he publish them for you?"

Badger could now see a strength in Mary that she hadn't often exhibited in the few days he had actually been in her company, and he liked it.

"Jurgenson didn't publish my book; he printed it. His money was in no way involved, but he made a good deal of lucre by doing the printing. It is a common, and legitimate practice for printers to include in their contracts a ten percent over or under printing cost. That is, their machines may print ten percent over or ten percent under the specified number of books. The buyer, as a result, pays the printer more or less than the contract, depending on the production. I've found out his company, always prints 10% over."

Mary, not to be undaunted, pushed on. "Well, what about that Mr. Zinecor? He seems okay."

"I do wish I knew what to say about Mr. Jack or John Zinecor. All I know about him is that he teaches languages at Goodman College, does translations and is unmarried but, according to George, spends his money on books. What I've observed is a man trying too hard to please Graham, and I wonder why. I also wonder, if he is as good a translator as George says, why doesn't he have a great deal more money?"

"I wonder, at times, Johnny, where is your Christian charity?" said Blanche. "I think you should wait until you have a reason to condemn someone."

"I'll just say that I think Zinecor goes along with the rest of the group and I don't trust them."

Bernadine looked up at the clock above the door. "Oh, my, aren't we having a gay afternoon."

Four chairs glided over the floor in such unison as to suggest Daniel Barenboim were conducting.

❦   ❦   ❦

CHAPTER IX

GOOD FRIDAY AFTERNOON

Our spring on the Hill I remember
even in the driest year of my life
        "The Spring on the Hill," Knute Skinner

Leaving the building was a good deal easier than entering it had been. The stairway was absent of any students and most of the police had gone. In the parking lot there was only one state police car and one with "Walden Police" painted on the front door. Wash Rutan was on the job. There were, however, a number of other cars about.

Mary and Blanche again led the parade down the sidewalk toward Lueker Hall, and Badger once more held Bernadine's arm. Two crows barked at them from an elm tree. An acute sense of smell, a swelling sensation in the stomach, followed by a chill, overcame Badger, the same feeling he sometimes experienced as a boy when he was left alone in his dark bedroom. It was on such a Stygian evening that his mother died. He had had the feeling several times afterward, often just before something unpleasant happened to him or to someone he loved. He tried to quicken the pace, but Bernadine was enjoying the campus beauty and wasn't inclined to speed up even if her legs and lungs had allowed it. Mary and Blanche reached Lueker Hall and waited for them. The four entered the building together. Nothing seemed amiss, but Badger couldn't shake the feeling that something bad had or was about to happen.

"Oh, Mr. Smith, I have a message for you." said the young man behind the desk. A police sergeant wants you to call him on his phone. He ripped off the top sheet from a note pad and gave it to Badger. Badger read the note. It had Sgt. Reburg's name on it and a telephone number that Badger recognied as being for a cellular.

He did what it always irritated him to see other do. He asked if he could use the phone while reaching behind the desk and taking it. The student clerk didn't even bother to answer, as Badger already had begun dialing. The three ladies waited with forbearance while Badger drummed the fingers of his free hand on the desk top and listened to the maniacal sounds of man's progressive electronic age. After a piercing four notes and a mechanical voice telling him he had made a mistake, he dialed again, this time with greater care and greater success.

"Sgt. Reburg here."

"Chuck, this is Badger."

"Badger. Glad you called. Please come upstairs to Room 247 in Lueker Hall right away. There's been another murder. One of the students says this is one of the classrooms you use." Badger heard a click and a buzz before he had a chance to ask who was murdered.

Patience is a virtue for only so long, and enough time had passed. Badger's aunts asked in unison, "What is it, Johnny?" while Mary mearly thought it.

"Another murder. This time in my classroom, just upstairs in this building. Reburg hung up before I could ask who it was."

It is said by those moronic enough to sniff cocaine that it gives a stimulation to body and mind unmatched in this tiny little world. These foolish people have never observed Aunt Bernadine and Blanche being told of a murder close by. Compassion for the family and friends of the deceased could, should, and would come later, but for now there was mystery and intrigue. Bernadine's aches and pains disappeared as she and Blanche turned without a word and looked for the staircase. Seeing it, they took on the speed of race horses. A smiling Mary and Badger were only a few steps behind.

A state policeman met the four on the landing, where he had been occupied keeping a few curious students from climbing any further. He escorted the four up to a classroom with a door marked 247, then turned and went back down the hall to arrest the progress of the curious students. While Badger turned the knob on the door all three ladies noticed that above that door hung a wooden plank with an inscription burned into it:

"All ye who enter here abandon Hopefully."

"Is that yours, Johnny?" asked Bernadine. Badger smiled. "I thought so."

"Actually I got it from Edward Newman. I doubt he'll mind."

Inside the room were numerous police checking everything. In the center front lay a corpse, its feet protruding from several plastic, green garbage bags. Several student desks had been pushed or knocked out of the way. Reburg, standing up behind the teacher's platformed desk, came forward.

"Didn't take you long to get here." He stepped over to the body and turned his back on the women, shielding them from a view of the corpse as he lifted one garbage bag enough to show Badger a view of the head.

"Oh my God, Zinecor!" said Badger.

Bernadine and Blanche out flanked Reburg and caught a good view of the head. It was turned slightly so the open eyes seemed to be staring at a large poster next to the blackboard. Reburg pulled the bag lower, not noticing the ladies. A sweatered chest, with a small hole and powder burns on the left side showed the cause of death.

"We'll wait for the autopsy, but I'd say it was a twenty-two shell. Looks like the barrell was pressed against his chest."

"Isn't a twenty-two rather small to kill a man?" asked Blanche.

"Not at all, Mam, I mean, Blanche. A twenty-two has some limitations, but at close range it kills just as dead as a forty-five and it's much easier to carry around.

"What can you tell us?" asked Badger.

"Not much to tell. Somebody downstairs heard 'a pop,' as she called it, and notified us. The explosion must have made quite a noise with all this hard wood, but the insulation between the floor and ceiling would have dampened it quite a bit. Since there was only one person who seems to have heard anything we can say that the workmanship here was first rate. Any way, one of my men came up here to investigate, found the door open, and found the body. We've checked all the rooms. There's no one on the floor. Found nothing that would help."

"How long ago was this?" asked Badger.

"About an hour." The sergeant's voice had a slight edge to it.

Mary left the group and wandered over to the poster at which the blind eyes seemed to be staring. She saw a large piece of tag board on which was neatly printed: 'Hopefully the sun will shine." Arrows identified word relationships. Below this was the note:

" 'Hopefully' is an adverb modifying the verb 'will shine.' Since the sun in incapable of shining with hope, the sentence is meaningless - as are almost all other sentences using the word 'hopefully.' Generally the speaker means 'I hope,' and that is what he would say if he ever thought before speaking. Caution: Hold suspect any person beginning a sentence with 'Hopefully' or pausing at the end then adding it."

"You like my penmanship?" She turned around to see Badger smiling at her, and back by the body, Bernadine and Blanche were giving Chuck Reburg a third degree.

"You certainly make a strong point. I'm not so sure that I would like to be one of your students, with the paraphrase from Dante's *Inferno* over the door and then this. What happens to a student if he does use 'hopefully?' Do you send him to the nether world?"

"Not quite so drastic as that. I embarrass him."

"That could be dangerous for you. You make them angry."

"True," said Badger, taking Mary's arm and leading her back to Bernadine and Blanche. "But most of my students are intellegent, and intelligent students when embarrassed, become angry at themselves and learn from it. Only the dull students become angry with me."

Chuck Reburg was scratching his black hair and looking down at Blanche who was entertaining with a bit of doggerel.

Murder Mystery

Profound as any Melville novel,
It raises hairs behind my ears;
And if I'm left alone to grovel ,
It shows me new and groundless fears.

Bernadine and Reburg laughed as Mary and Badger joined them. It would be inaccurate to say that the still uncovered Jack Zinecor laughed, although Blanche was pleased to notice a slight curling upward of his lips.

"There can't be any possible question that this death is related to that of Larry Sermons and the book thefts, but I certainly don't know what that relationship is," said Chuck Reburg. "Any idea, Mr. Smith, why Zinecor was in your classroom or even why the door wasn't locked?"

"None whatever, *Chuck.* " Badger put great emphasis on the sergeant's first name. "There is one thing, however, to keep in mind; I'm not the only teacher who uses this room, nor is this the only room that I teach in."

Reburg drew a deap breath and pulled out a note pad with an attached pencil. "I'd appreciate the names of everyone else who teaches in here?"

"Let's see . . . Ken Ettner, the department chairman meets both his senior seminar class here and his Shakespeare class . . . and also his freshman communications class."

"He in town, you know?" asked the sergeant.

"Won't be back until Sunday, late." said Badger. Besides Ken there's Alice Pragman. She teaches English lit. and also the modern novel and, of course, communications. Alice is in town. I saw her just the other day."

Reburg wrote down the name on his pad. "She live in town or on campus?" Badger pointed toward town. "Right. How come your department chairman teaches a freshman course?

"At Carlton-Stokes, and probably every small college in the country, everybody teaches the freshmen. There are more freshmen than anything else. Drop out rate, you see. Communications is our version of composition, only we add speech and make it a four hour course rather than three. The paper work is heavy so we all do it. Outside our department, Edmund Linehan uses the room for his class in something late in the afternoon, and I'm sure that Coral Reiser is using it this semester for music history or something."

Reburg wrote down the names. "I'll see Prof. Linehan in his office in a little while. You happen to know where Coral Reiser or Alice Pragman live?" Badger didn't know Alice Pragman's address and could give only vague directions to Coral Reiser's apartment.

Bernadine and Blanche walked about the room, happy to have a chance to see where their Johnny taught English. Mary soon followed. They stopped by a large window and looked out at the Mississippi River and the State of Illinois just beyond it. After a few moments Bernadine looked down at the church and the steps below. She turned around and looked at Reburg.

"Chuck!" She observed all of the policemen. "Sgt. Reburg, I think I know why this room was used."

Every one of the policemen in the room was looking at her. Chuck Reburg, followed by Badger, stepped over to the window. Bernadine nodded at the sergeant who looked out at the Mississippi and finally down at the church and steps below. A puzzled frown filled his face.

"Don't you see?" said Bernadine, "This is a perfect place to watch for someone coming up the Hill."

They looked out on the long, narrow, wooden steps that lead up to the college. "I stare out this window every day for the beauty of the view. It was just too much with me," said Badger.

"Well, 'The World is too much with us, late and soon.'" quoted Blanche. "I realize I should have said, 'Too much light often blinds gentlemen of this sort. They cannot see the forest for the trees,' but Wordsworth is always so much more beautiful than Christoph Wieland, don't you think?"

Everyone smiled, then slowly began edging his way toward the door. It was obvious that there was nothing more that could be done here. Mary took Badger by the hand and pulled him back a bit.

"When my husband was murdered this past Christmas you tied in everything to something you had read. Do you see any allusions to either of these murders to anything at all in your reading?"

Badger smiled and kept hold of Mary's hand as they followed Bernadine and Blanche out the door and back down to the first floor. He didn't say a word until they were in front of the check-in desk. The male student had been replaced by a coed who smiled at everyone, and waited. Her appearance told Badger that it was getting late in the afternoon. At the same time, his taste buds told him it was now dangerously close to the cocktail hour.

"The subject of allusions I plan to take up just as soon as we get our tonsils lubricated," Badger told Mary. "It sounds as if I'm planning to give a lecture, doesn't it?" Mary smiled.

"I had my tonsils taken out when I was but a wee slip of a girl," said Blanche. "Do you suppose it would be all right if I moistened my epiglottis instead?"

❦   ❦   ❦

CHAPTER X

GOOD FRIDAY EVENING

In the rain the trees overcome me.
                    "Changes," Marvin Bell
The green horse of the tree
bucks in the wind
                    "Storm," Lucien Stryk

"Old Man River" does a great deal more than just keep rolling along, despite what Oscar Hammerstein wrote. The Mississippi picks up little insignificant dew drops in Minnesota, whips up a wind in Wisconsin and Iowa and drops a heavy rain on Illinois and Missouri before the television weatherman has had time to apologize for his poor prophesies of the day. But before the news, weather, and sports can be digested, the rain has moved to the next county, leaving only puddles, wet grass, and drooping trees.

The rain had just started when the four would-be detectives arrived at Badger's apartment house. They were only slightly damp when they reached the top of the stairs and entered the living room, the door to which was being held open by George.

"I was just watching those trees over there in the park begin to take on qualities of bogey men when you drove up. I was hoping to see them snatch up some of those crows who flew under them to stay dry. No matter. They'll get into somebody's garbage soon enough and poison themselves." George sat back down by the window.

"My, aren't we being gruesome, George! This doesn't sound like you at all," said Bernadine, trying to catch her breath. "I had imagined you to be a defender of all our feathered friends."

The three ladies took the same seats they had had the evening before while Badger stepped around the bookcase to the kitchen and began slicing cheese.

"I apologize, Bernadine, and to you Blanche and Mary, as well. I'm sure I never wished any harm upon any creature, before today."

"And what happened on this day that has turned you into the phantom of the osprey? asked Blanche. "That is, if I may be so bold to ask, which I have already done."

"Oh, it's Coral, Miss Reiser. I'm afraid that I don't understand women at all. I thought that we had something of an understanding, but apparently we don't. While I was at her apartment the phone rang and she accepted an invitation to have dinner with Graham Carruth. Graham Carruth!"

Badger could be heard in the kitchen making beautiful sounds with ice and crystal and some liquid, sounds that rivaled Mozart's *Eine Kleine Nachtmusik*. Moments later he turned the corner and entered his living room carrying a tray with a pitcher of manhattans, three empty glasses and two lowball glasses filled with martinis on the rocks. He set the tray down on the coffee table and reached over to the top of the bookcase, where he had placed the large platter of cheese and crackers. He set the platter on the table next to the tray of drinks. The ritual continued.

"Did you happen to hear where they were going to dinner?" asked Badger.

George picked up one of the martinis and took a long pull, not waiting for the ladies' drinks to be poured. "I can't see where that matters a bit, but yes, they are going to the Lanai Room on Fourth St. in Quincy."

"Actually it matters a great deal," said Badger, pouring the ladies' drinks then sitting down next to Mary. "If Graham were taking her to his home I would be a bit concerned for you, but since they are going to a public - and expensive restaurant I would say that Graham thinks he can get some information from Coral, and Coral accepted his invitation only because she thought she could learn something from him." He sounded more sure of himself than he actually was.

"Do you really think so? Then Coral is trying to help us in this murder mystery. What a girl!" George took another long pull from his martini, but this time with greater satisfaction. "I sure hope she'll be safe, what with all the books stolen and a man murdered already."

"I really don't think you have to worry about Coral with Mr. Carruth," said Mary. I think Coral can handle any number of people like him. And didn't you know? There has been a second murder."

The first round of drinks was consumed to the accompanyment of explanations of Jack Zinecor's murder and what had been learned on the Hill that afternoon, much the same as the recurring theme in Rimsky-Korsakoff's *Scheherezade*. Badger placed the empty pitcher and two glasses on the tray and started for the kitchen.

"I've been so occupied with Zinecor's death that I completely forgot about dinner. I guess we will have to go out to eat," he said as he laid the tray down on the kitchen counter.

George looked up and then called over the bookcase into the kitchen, "If your legendary powers of observation were as great in daily life as they are in criminal situations you might have noticed that your stove is turned on low and that there is a large bowl of tossed salad in the refrigerator that would have been impossible for a normal person to miss when going for ice." He looked at the three women and lowered his voice. "I fixed the dinner last night before going to bed, brought it over and popped it in the oven and tossed a salad just before you arrived."

"What epicurean delight have you prepared for us tonight?" asked Bernadine.

"I thought that because today is Friday, so no meat for you, and the anniversary of Beethoven's birth, we should indulge in the maestro's favorite dish, Macaroni and cheese."

"We all love macaroni and cheese," said Mary, "and I have heard that it was Beethoven's favorite dinner; however I think you will find that Beethoven's birthday was in December, just after Christmas, not in April."

Badger returned with the filled pitcher and the two martinis. "Touche, Mary. You've struck George in the heart. He's been using the Beethoven gambit for as long as I've known him, all as an excuse to serve his special macaroni and cheese, which needs no excuse whatsoever." He poured the three ladies' drinks and waited for the appearance of the cigarettes, his lighter at the ready.

"Now that we have another special meal to look forward to, I suggest that we get back to the subject of the missing books and the two murders," said Bernadine, taking a puff on her cigarette and blowing smoke from her mouth before pronouncing the last three words.

"I agree," said Blanche, with that twinkle in her eye that was seldom missing. "After all, Johnny, I have moisened my epiglottis as promised and now wish to hear you elucidate on all or some of the awesome happenings in terms of the allusions you promised Mary a little while ago.

Badger took out a cigarette and started to light it. "I am going to cut down, not tomorrow, as I tell myself every day, but right now." He replaced the cigarette in the package. "You want allusions, I'll give you allusions and a few illusions. "Isn't 'Wash' the perfect name for our town marshall? Do you remember Sherwood Anderson's Wash in *Winesburg, Ohio* ?" He said this to no one in particular. "Anderson describes him as being the ugliest man in town. Now isn't that a fitting name for Marshall Rutan? Ugly inside and out!"

"Johnny, you're being very un-Christian on this most Christian of week-ends. This is Good Friday," said Blanche. "I'm sure the marshall is good to his mother and any aunts he may have. But pray go on, Dear. Don't stop. We would like to hear more of your theories."

Badger had been around his two aunts often enough to know and understand their special type of criticism or put down, to use the venacular, as had Mary. George, however, was a bit taken aback.

"I believe I understand the mystery of the forged versus the stolen books and, as a consequence, the motive for Larry Sermons' murder," Badger began. I believe Larry was paid to place the forged books in the Archives and remove the original volumes, as I said before."

"What makes you think that? There's no proof." said George.

"No, but some very good hearsay and circumstantial evidence. Sermons was known widely on our Mississippi as a Duke or Dolphin, take your pick. Anyone who was interested in having some petty crime committed would think of Sermons right away. His reputation extended beyond our little hamlet of Walden, so that he was probably known to everyone who is even remotely connected to this case. What I am saying is this: Someone wanted those books, the ones that were replaced by forgeries, made the forgeries and paid Sermons to make the switches, either all at once or one at a time. I favor one at a time. Larry realized that there was big money involved and decided to do a little extra-curricular stealing. Since he knew absolutely nothing about books, he stole ones that looked to be valuable."

"Yes, Johnny," broke in Bernadine. "That has happened a number of times. Blanche, remember the Iversons who used to live below us?" When Blanche nodded Bernadine looked at everyone in the room. "Ted Iverson bought several hundred books at an auction for just a few dollars. As soon as he got them home he called Blanche and me to his apartment. He was positive he had a fortune in books. Remember, Blanche? What he had were some very nice books that were worth just about what he paid for them, but because the books were old he assumed they were valuable."

Blanche smiled. "I remember that his wife, Vivian, picked up a copy of *Green Mansions* and opened it to the back of the title page and showed me that it was a first edition and should have great value. It was a first edition all right, a first edition of one of the many American editions. Just a reprint. These were educated, intelligent people. If they could be fooled then....."

"Exactly," said Badger. "Larry Sermons was certainly not your Vivian and Ted Iverson, so he took books that he was sure had value and that he could sell quickly for a profit. Whether or not he actually tried to sell the books is difficult to say at this time, but I'm sure that when the county wakes up and Chuck Reburg can get a warrant he'll find the missing books in Sermon's home or apartment or woodshed or whatever. That explains why we have two different types of thefts. One was the valuable books that someone paid Sermons to steal and replace with the forgeries and the second was the books Sermons stole outright."

Mary took a small sip from her drink, opened her mouth to speak, then closed it again.

"Were you going to say something, Mary?" asked Blanche. "Don't let Johnny intimidate you. He's a big softy at heart."

"Yes, I was. I have a question, Johnny. I'm sorry, Badger. Actually, I have two. Can't the police go into the home of a murdered man without a warrant? I would sure think they could. And if Larry Sermons stole some of the books why do you think they would still be in his possession and not sold, sold to the very person who paid him to take the other books? I grant you they were not of great value, but most of them did have some worth."

Badger gave Mary a smile that most critics of the cinema would say was straight out of *Now, Voyager.* I don't really know anything about warrants, but I do know that last year the state police got into a great deal of trouble when they went into the Bauman Home over by the lake and a short time later their son reported several dozen valuable pieces of antique glass ware missing. It turned out that the antiques were in their other home, but the police have been very careful since then. As for your other question: "True, Mary. Many people would be happy to pay even an extravagant amount for, say, the Robinson book, but if the forger wanted the book he would have used his same method, not changed it. It's possible some of the books were sold to somebody else, but not all of them and certainly not *The Hill* !"

"Why then was this Larry Sermons murdered?" asked Bernadine, looking at Badger and then at everyone else. "Do you have a theory on that?"

"Because he destroyed the forger's plan, which was to have Sermons take the various works from the Archies and leave forged copies or counterfeits in their place. The forger was sure that nothing would have been noticed until years later. But Sermons stole some books outright, and Graham spotted the missing books and because of it, the forgeries. The situation was known to a great many before Sermons' death. My guess is that the forger went to the Archives to have it out with Sermon, and, in a fit of anger, killed him."

"That makes some sense," said Bernadine, but, as we all know, murder doesn't always make sense, at least not the kind of sense that we understand. And what about the new murder, Johnny?"

Badger took a long pull from his drink, took out a cigarette and almost lit it, then smiled and returned the coffin nail to the pack. "At this point that is a tough one. Jack Zinecor knew a great deal about books and had quite a large collection, according to Graham. He was either somehow involved in the thefts or somehow found out who was and so was murdered."

"Zinecor is such an unusual name," said Blanche. "It sounds like the medicine I take for cholesterol at breakfast."

"Speaking of meal time, I had better do a few things if we are going to eat tonight," said George, getting up and going to the kitchen. "Beethoven's favorite dinner will be ready in less than ten minutes. The noodles will take little time; however the five cheeses Beethoven and I use take a bit longer."

Bernadine looked over where Badger's double bass violin was leaning against the wall. "Perhaps, Johnny, if you played something for us, you would be able to solve the mystery, the way Sherlock Holmes does sometimes with his violin."

"You should have your Johnny play the string

quartet he has been writing," said George, leaning his head over the bookcase.

"Oh, Badger, a string quartet! We'd love to hear it," said Mary.

"Yes, Johnny, we would all love to hear it!" sang Bernadine and Blanche in perfect harmony.

Badger gave George an irritated glance then looked at the three ladies. "Even if I had the considerable talent of a Gary Carr I doubt that I would be able to play a string quartet on a bass violin."

"Of course, dear," said Bernadine, "but you could tell us about it. Is it the conventional instruments or is there a bass in the group?"

Badger smiled and winked at his aunt. "No, it is conventional, two violins, a viola, and a cello; however I am requiring that the four musicians use only German bows, no French bows."

John Badger Smith's favorite joke elicited not even one curled lip from his listeners as the four talked on until George announced that dinner was served, and entered with the silverware.

CHAPTER XI

GOOD FRIDAY NIGHT

1 wanted spring to make me gasp for breath
to make me ache in root and branch.
                    "Ask Me Now,"   Dave Etter

𝕬 clap of thunder followed by the sounds
of rain on the roof and against the front window pane
informed the little group of arm chair detectives (Or
perhaps the term should be couch and straight chair
detectives?) that the clean spring rain had not stopped
this early Friday evening, which was turning into night,
as   the shadows were quickly slipping into darkness.
The   meal was now over and a tired   and frustrated
George Mercater was ready to leave, to follow Miss
Coral Reiser to the ends of whatever it was that would
bring her to him. He hurriedly   packed up his utensils,
left over cheeses, and his now empty casserole bowl
and left.

Badger saw his friend George down to his car
while the three ladies, who in most romantic narratives
would be called "girls," dried the remaining dishes.
Mary leaned   back against the kitchen side of the
bookcase and rubbed her eyes.   "I'm not sure who it is,
but Coral Reiser certainly reminds me of someone in
something I've read, an English novel perhaps."

"The Return of the Native, " said Blanche.
"Miss Reiser is a very handsome person,   I'm sure
you must be thinking of Eustacia Vye.   Just look in

her very stern and determined eye. Oh, if Johnny were here, I made a rhyme!"

"Indeed you did, Blanche," said Bernadine, "but I think I would have thought of Miss Reiser not so much with Thomas Hardy as with Jane Austin. She reminds me of Emma, so beautiful and clever and so on, whatever so on means."

"Who reminds you of whom?" asked Badger, coming in the door, slightly out of breathe.

"It is very disrespectful for young men to listen in on their elders and then interrogate them on any subject, much less one that may have the slight stigma of *yenta*, as some of my friends back at the library might say," answered Bernadine before Badger had had a chance to plop into a chair. "When we want you to know something we will tell you."

Badger looked lovingly at his aunt. How many people in the civilized world had people they could talk to like this? "Since you cannot be discussing Mary because she is right here, you must be talking about Coral. Clever deduction?"

"Very deft!" said Blanche, "but you missed something. Mary and Bernadine were discussing me, in the third person. You will admit that 'beautiful and clever' fit me to a tee, as many of the golfers say."

"Some golfers are apt to say almost anything," said Badger, "But, true, you are both beautiful and clever."

Blanche put down her dish rag and came into the living room and gave Badger a hug and kiss, then whispered a bit of parental love in his ear before going back to the kitchen side of the room. Badger sat for a minute before saying or doing anything. Finally he kicked his feet out and stretched.

"Back to my clever deduction. I am sure that you see more in Coral than beautiful and clever. What had you been saying about her?"

"If you must know," said Mary, "I had said that Coral reminded me of someone in something I had read. Blanche suggested that it might be Eustacia Vye, while Bernadine thought she was more like Jane Austin's Emma. I'm not at all sure that either of those two really fit, but . . ."

"Mary forgot the most important part," interrupted Blanche. "I said she was like Eustacia Vye because she had a very stern and determined eye. Could you make a rhyme as good as that one, Johnny?"

"No, I don't think so. For only if I should give way to delusion could there be a suitable rhyming allusion."

"I think I may have been thinking of Bessie, the model, in *The Light that Failed.*"

"Whatever or whomever you were thinking of," said Badger, "Coral reminds every one of us of someone who is presently not good for George. This is strange, because until this business of the date with Graham came up I believe that Coral was the perfect person for George."

The three women talked about George and

Coral until they had dried all the dishes and came back into the living area and sat down. Badger had been thumbing through a thin, green paper bound volume, no bigger than his own published poems. He put the book down, went to the kitchen and returned with four brandy snifters and a half filled bottle on a tray.

"I have an idea," said Badger, as he poured from the bottle. "I'm not sure it is smart of me to tell you three what it is, but no one ever accused me of being smart." Since the room was filled with silence, Badger continued. "The police are afraid to go into Larry Sermons' quarters and search for books until they can get a search warrant. The murderer just might take this opportunity to sneak into Sermons' place tonight and remove anything that he wouldn't want to be found."

"What makes you think that, Johnny?" said Bernadine. "He could have broken into Mr. Sermons' home any time after he killed him."

"I don't think so. I did a little checking in this college directory." Badger held up the slim green volume. "And Sermons is listed as living in a room over by the Methodist church. His landlady, a Mrs. Helen Watgen, would certainly have discovered by now if anyone broke in last night or before, and no one would have broken in today in the daylight. I think the murderer has had a chance to think things out and very likely will want to look around."

"What about Jack Zinecor?" Mary asked. "It seems to me that the murderer should be just as interested in searching his home in Quincy as he would be in searching Larry Sermons' rented room here in town, maybe even more so since Mr.

Zinecor's death is more recent." She looked at Badger but took in Bernadine and Blanche with her gestures.

"True, Mary" said Badger, "but I don't think the police in Quincy, Illinois, will be as skiddish as they are here in Missouri, or at least as skiddish as one Sgt. Charles Reburg seems to have become. When I talked to him alone while you three were looking out the window and Bernadine noticed what a good observation post the room was, he seemed like a different person from the one I was getting to like so much. Something has happened with him? But getting back to your point, Mary, I think the Quincy police will have checked Zinecor's home just as soon as they were notified of the death."

"I agree about the sergeant," said Blanche. "He became very formal, especially with you, Johnny."

"If you will indulge me, I would like to leave you alone here for a little while while I go over to Sermons' apartment. I think that Mrs. Watgen will let me in, since I am the official representative of the college this week." Badger lifted the brandy bottle and looked at it. "I think there is enough to hold you until I return."

"I think that is a good idea, Badger," said Mary, "but I think that I should come with you. This Mrs. Watgen is much more likely to let you into Larry Sermons' room if you are accompanied by a woman than if you are alone."

"That's a very good idea," Bernadine said. "Blanche and I will feel much better about it if you have someone with you. Mary can protect you in case of any trouble you might run into."

"Besides," said Blanche, "That will leave more brandy for us."

*　　*　　*

Mary and Badger got out of Badger's Ford Taurus and walked up the walk leading to the trim little cottage close to the Methodist church. When Badger rang the bell there was an immediate deep bark and soon after the door opened and a trim lady in her fifties opened the door. Badger started to explain what they wanted, but Mary broke in, and soon the woman opened the door wide and they entered. The dog, for it was indeed a dog who had barked, rubbed his side against Badger's leg, leaving a generous supply of hair as a token of friendship. He was large and very, very old, undoubtedly the inspiration for all of the shaggy dog stories that have ever been told. The four went to the back of the house, where Larry Sermons had spent many hours of his life staring at the ceiling, as the room had nothing in it except a bed, a chair, and a chest of drawers. After checking under and behind the bed, and behind the dresser Badger opened each of the drawers and checked the contents carefully while Mary kept the landlady occupied in conversation. He then opened the closet door and went through all the pants and coat pockets and even kicked at the three pairs of shoes on the floor. A number of boxes on the shelf contained all sorts of rubble, from old cigarette lighters, to a broken pocket radio, pieces of rusted metal, and book matches, nothing that told him anything new about the man who had lived there.

Mary and Badger, joined by the landlady and the dog, went out of the room. As Badger shut the door he noticed how the street light shone on the empty bed and the army blanket that acted as a spread.

"Larry usually spent part of every day lying on the bed with all his clothes on," the woman said. "I used to say to him: 'Larry you aught to go down to the library and get yourself something good to read,' but he just said that reading was for fools and little girls. I'm sure sorry Larry got killed. He may not have been the most popular man in town, but he was a good roomer; always paid his rent on time, an' never smoked in his room." Mary had gone out to stand by the car and look up at the clearing sky while Badger and the woman stood by the entry door, the dog still rubbing against Badger's leg. "I wonder why anyone would want to kill him?"

"That's what we're all trying to find out. Well, good-night, Mrs. Watgen," Badger said.

"Oh, I'm not Mrs. Watgen," the woman said. "I'm Mrs. Schmidt, Beverly Schmidt. Mrs. Watgen sold this place to me last year and moved up near Chicago somewhere. Larry just stayed on."

"Well, good-night, Mrs. Schmidt," Badger said.

"Good-night," the woman said.

Badger walked to the car feeling as if he had just played Nick Adams in a dramatization of Hemingway's "The Killers." Mary stood looking at the sky with her back to him but heard his footfalls.

" 'Night hath a thousand eyes,' " she said, "but very few this night. Did you learn anything in there?"

The two got in the car and Badger drove up

the road a few blocks then turned left before attempting any answer. It was taking him some time to clear the Nick Adams image from his mind.

"I can't be sure but I think something was taken from the room. There was just a hint of dust under the bed and it looked as though something may have been scraped across the floor."

"While you were looking here and there I talked to Mrs. Watgen and she. . . . ."

"I found out that wasn't Mrs. Watgen; she sold the place a year ago to this lady, Mrs. Schmidt, I think she said, but Sermons stayed on."

"Well then, Mrs. Schmidt told me that a young man, she thought it might be a college student, was here shortly before we came and said that he was supposed to pick up some things in a box from Larry Sermons' room. She wouldn't let him in. He went off up the street in the direction of the college. She watched him until he was out of sight. Does that suggest anything to you?"

Badger steered his Taurus over the wet street, enjoying the many reflections the occasional street lights made in the frequent puddles. "It would have been easy for that person to double back and get into Sermons' room by the window. I noticed it was not locked. I doubt Mrs. Schmidt's evaluation that it was a college student. A college student would be too easy to find and trace to the person who sent him on the arrend, especially tonight when there are so few students on campus. My guess is that it was one of the many farm boys in the area. I don't imagine Mrs. Schmidt gave you a physical description of the boy."

"Sometimes John Badger Smith, you are really insufferable. What you meant to say was 'I don't imagine you were alert enough to ask for a physical description.' It just so happens that I did. I even wrote it down." Mary opened her purse and took out a little note pad. She waited until Badger had pulled up in front of his dwelling and turned off the motor. She opened the door and the dome light came on, giving just enough light to read her notes. "Mrs. Schmidt thought he was about five feet nine or ten with very blond hair that almost looked bleached. She thinks his eyes were blue. He had on a pair of blue jeans and multi-colored sport shirt. His shoes were brown and muddy. That's why she wouldn't let him step over the threshhold. His voice, she said, was strong but rather high."

The two got out of the car and walked into the house and up the steps. They could hear Bernadine and Blanche saying a rosary. When they walked in the door the two older women stood up and hugged the returning native and Mary. Badger noticed that they had not touched their brandy since he and Mary had left some time before.

"We've just three 'Hail Marys' and an 'Act of Contrition' to go," said Blanche. "We'll be right with you."

The two ladies continued their prayers with Bernadine saying the first part and Blanche answering after "the fruit of thy womb, Jesus." The simple scene encouraged Badger and Mary to join Blanche as they quietly took seats. When the prayers were finished Badger poured a bit of brandy into each of their two empty snifters then he and Mary filled in his aunts on what they had learned on their short excursion to Sermons' room.

"I really don't imagine that the boy who came to the door took anything from the room," said Bernadine. "If he climbed in the window with muddy shoes on he would have left tracks, and I doubt that he would have taken his shoes off. It seems out of character for a thief or messenger or, for that matter, any adolescent in this modern world of ours. "

"Which would mean that the marks under the bed have nothing to do with this case, is that what you mean, Bernadine?" Badger asked.

"Or it might mean that this Mrs. Schmidt took something from under the bed," said Blanche. "The story of the college boy might have been a bit of equivocation to throw you off the track, that is if you could ever find a woman who would lie. Maybe she took something belonging to her lodger in order to have something to remember him by. Remember what you said about him, that he was a good tenant. Maybe she had a crush on him."

CHAPTER XII

LATE GOOD FRIDAY NIGHT

The woman named Tomorrow
Sits with a hatpin in her teeth
And takes her time
    "Four Preludes on Playthings of the Wind,"
                      Carl Sandburg

Bernadine and Blanche had been in bed a long time when Badger escorted Mary back to the student union from a walk over the entire college campus, including what was referred to as the back campus. The football stadium was located there, and a wooded area stood beyond, where students for years had been discovering love. It was in the wooded area that Mary Mallony and John Badger Smith discovered what Badger's aunts had known for some time, that their strong liking for each other was indeed love, a love that meant wedlock. They discussed openly their previous marriages, Badger's, whose ended tragically in a car accident some years before, and Mary's, whose ended in murder the Christmas season just past. They both knew that they wanted their lives to be together.

"Will you always love me?" Mary had asked.

"Always," answered Badger.

"Then I guess we're engaged. Who was it who wrote the song 'Love Never Went to College'?"

"That was Rodgers and Hart from *Too Many*

Girls. Why? Do you think love isn't smart?"

"I don't know. It's just that love certainly came to this college and made me wiser."

"It made both of us wiser."

Mary laughed. The two kissed again then started walking hand in hand both humming the Richard Rodgers melody.

"Are you sure you want to marry me?"

Mary nodded.

"Good!" said Badger.

They returned to the union in a state of euphoria, almost giving in to the temptation to wake the Badger sisters to give them the news. It wasn't the power of cold reason that kept them from it. It was the kind heart of Mary, realizing that Bernadine and Blanche needed sleep, in part because the woman named Tomorrow had donned her hat and was on her way. The two lovers kissed, held each other very close, kissed again, and parted, She going into her room and he starting down the campus Hill to his apartment on foot.

Badger paid little attention to where he was walking, as his thoughts were on Mary and what he saw of their lives together. He noticed that he was not going straight to his apartment, but had veered off toward the Methodist church. He stopped thinking about Mary and took up the subject of the marks under the bed and the possibility that someone, the boy described to Mary or someone else, had gotten in through the unlocked window. Or Mrs. Schmidt . . . . .

The sound of his feet hitting the now dry pavement made an eerie, unnatural sound, and he felt somehow afraid that people would be awakened by it. He stepped over onto the lush grass and walked. The earlier rain had made the grass soggy and slowed his progress. Stepping back onto the sidewalk he made, at least what appeared to him to be, the sounds of Fred Astaire walking, a sound that was always the most beautiful dancing in all terpsichore.

He could see the Watgen - now the Schmidt - home ahead on his left. A number of automobiles lined the street, as garages were less common in Walden than barns and storage sheds. He moved into the shadows provided by the many trees and approached the window that he was sure had been Larry Sermons'. He walked slowly, examining the ground as he went, looking for footprints and being careful not to make any of his own, at least none that could later be identified. The wind that had earlier brought the downpour now rustled through the many trees, causing drops of rain to fall on his head and somewhat slumped shoulders in a fashion that suggested the wind was trying to anoint him.

He reached the window. There was just enough light from a street lamp to make out scuff marks on the ground below him. He took his lighter from his pocket and stooped over, hoping to get a clear indication of what had happened outside the window quite a few hours before.

A light flashed before him. He jumped to his right and hid behind a spiraea bush. The window was ablaze with a cold, bare light from the ceiling of the room beyond. Badger moved very slowly around the bush so that he could see better into what had been Larry Sermons' chamber. Soon he realized that with the light coming through the window, he could see in but no one in the room could see out at him unless he got too close. He had only to be careful of anyone looking out from the house behind him, an unlikely possibility. From his vantage point he could see little, a large piece of ceiling and the light, part of the bed post, and some shadows. He looked down at the ground directly below the window. The scuff marks were unmistakable footprints and scarred ground where the grass left off and the dirt, now drying mud, surrounded the bushes. The siding below the window had dirt and mud marks, and the window itself had smudges that very well might have been made by a person's hands. Badger looked back up at the window. He could discern several moving shadows made by human figures, not much beyond the doorway. In spite of himself, Badger shuddered. He felt like Tom Sawyer and Huck Finn when they saw the approaching figures in the graveyard. He was unaware of sound untll he heard his own name spoken in a high pitched woman's voice:

"Professor Smith from the college and a lovely lady were here some time ago. They looked the room over pretty carefully, at least Professor Smith did. I knew who he was. The girl next store was in his American Literature class or something and said he was a terrible grader, almost impossible to get an A in his class. Do you think that's right? I always say that I think the teachers and professors should give high grades to all the students . It would help to encourage the them to do better and think better of themselves; don't you think?"

"Certainly, especially in brain surgery."

"Oh, aren't you the card!"

Badger moved up under the sill and carefully lifted his head. There was Mrs. Schmidt in the doorway and beside her was...was... Sgt. Reburg. The sergeant moved about the room just as Badger himself had done several hours before. Was it an illusion or did Reburg have a smile on his face as he searched through the room? It was difficult to tell from Badger's vantage point.

"I was in my back sitting room doing some knitting, just as I was when you come to the door. I have trouble sleeping so I stay up and sew or knit. Recognized the professor right away, but the nice lady explained how they were involved in the case and how the professor was sort of in charge of the college over the spring break. I did the right thing, letting them in, I mean?"

"Sure, sure. There's no problem there. Did Professor Smith take anything from the room?"

"No, I watched him and he looked all around, but he didn't take anything. He opened the boxes just as you are doing, but nothing was taken. And the lady never really entered the room. She stood back by the door with me the whole time they was here.

"Are you sure? Sure he didn't slip something into his pocket or hold something behind his back?"

"Far as I could tell he left the room the same way he came. Why would a professor at the college want to take something out of Larry's room? From what

I saw, Prof. Smith was just checking, just like you are."

"Well, we have to be sure, Mrs. Watgen. Can't take chances.

"Oh, but I'm not Mrs. Watgen. I'm Mrs. Schmidt. Mrs. Watgen sold...." Badger was back with Hemingway.

He backed away from the window and, using the bushes for cover, waited along the side of the house. He could see the street and Reburg's police car, something he had missed earlier because he had been concentrating on the ground in front of him. A few moments later Reburg stepped out of the house and walked to his car. Badger was tempted to call to him and point out the marks below the window but decided not to. Reburg's strange behavior in the past few hours certainly suggested that someone higher up in the state police had put the fear of non-promotion in him and so he was acting too much like the type of cop who would not appreciate a layman butting in on his case..

Reburg's car moved off up the street. Once it was out of sight, Badger moved from behind the bushes and started back to his apartment, passing the Mu Theta house on the way, the fraternity for which he was the faculty advisor.

Why did Reburg wait so long before looking at Larry Sermons' room? Why did he wait until the middle of the night to inspect the place? Badger looked at his watch. Ten past one. Hardly the time to be calling on Mrs. Schmidt. And then, what about Coral Reiser? Her deportment was certainly strange. Did any of this have anything at all to do with the book thefts and the two murders or was Badger letting some unrelated behavior get in his way of thinking. None of this was anything like the murder of Mary's husband last Christmas. Mary! Badger was now on to a far more exciting subject. Mary! Marriage! A life with Mary. Seeing her the first thing every morning and the last thing every night. This kept Badger's mind occupied until he climbed the stairs, turned left and entered his living room.

He found the timer switch in the dark and turned on the light. On the couch, face up, lay George Mercater, fast asleep. Badger moved quietly to the kitchen and the refrigerator. The sound of milk filling a glass was too much for George and he woke up.

"Pour me a glass, too."

"It's milk, not gin."

"I know it's milk."

Badger reentered his small living room with two tall, red Texas tumblers, ten ounce plastic glasses, and laid them down on the top of the coffee table. George grabbed one of the glasses and gulped down half the contents.

"Just to satisfy my idle curiosity, George, why don't you tell me what you are doing here at." Badger looked at his watch. "At twenty-five minutes after one in the morning."

"I had an uncontrolable thirst for milk and my cat, Fluffy, just finished off the last quart in the house, so I came over here where I knew I would be treated cordially and given the *white* milk I so craved, in a *red* glass!"

Badger smiled at his friend, knowing full well that George's presence had something to do with Coral. "First of all, you are more likely to keep a poisonous viper in your domicile than a pussy cat named Fluffy, and secondly, you are never out of milk and buy it by the gallon, not the quart. Tell me about Coral." He sat down in his chair, turned it to face George and took a sip from his glass and waited.

"I acted like a school boy, like a silly grammar school lad who has a crush on his teacher. I drove over to Coral's apartment tonight and waited for them to get home from their dinner in Quincy. It was eleven-thirty when they finally drove up, pretty late for just going out to dinner, if you ask me. Then they sat in Graham's Ford until well after twelve o'clock. I was just mad enough to drag Graham out of his car and give him the beating of his life."

The picture of George inflicting pain on anyone was too much for Badger. He had to turn his head around so that George couldn't see his face. "I'm glad that you didn't give in to your violent side," he said between clenched teeth. What did you do?"

"I waited until I saw the light go on inside of Coral's apartment and until Graham's Ford had turned the corner. I was going to go up to Coral's door but thought better of it and drove on home. But I couldn't stand the silence, so I walked over here. You weren't here, as you probably know, so I made myself at home. That damned light went out on me so I just took a nap until you walked in on me. Where were you, anyway? Did you keep that poor little girl out all this time?"

Badger recounted his adventures of the evening starting with Mary and his aunts in this very room and ending with his betrothal to Mary.

"We can't possibly toast your coming nuptuals with milk. Did you and your lovely aunts drink up all your brandy? Fetch it out for a bit of celebration."

Badger gladly did as he was told and the two friends talked of love and marriage well into the night, or more accurately, well into the morning.

"You two should be married here in Walden," George said as in a revelation. "Mary no longer has any ties to Oak Meadow except your aunts. And I believe they would love another trip down here. I'm sure that her priest there would gladly give up his claim to officiate at her wedding. You could be married at the end of the semester. I never did believe in long engagements. And I'm sure you won't either when you realize that in a few days you will be here teaching while she is back in Oak Meadow. Sounds like a good plan, doesn't it?"

"It sounds like an excellent plan, George, except for one little detail. Our church is scheduled for major renovation at the end of May, just when our semester would be ending. Father McLaughlin will be saying masses in La Grange down the highway. I, and I'm sure Mary, have no desire to be married in a strange town."

George smiled the smile of intrigue. "You could be married in the chapel on campus."

"Father McLaughlin is a liberal, and, I understand, so is Bishop Roberts, in St. Louis, but I doubt if either one would allow a Catholic marriage to take place in a chapel of the Christian Disciples."

"I really don't see why not. Father McLaughlin has delivered a sermon every year at one of our Wednesday chapel sessions. I can't think of a major denomination that hasn't been represented."

"That's true, but delivering a sermon is quite different from performing a marriage. Also, I'm not at all sure that the faculty and staff would appreciate a disruption in the classroom building during the time of final exams."

"Now there you have a point," admitted George. He remained silent for some time, then stretched out on the couch. "The solution to that one is easy. You get married in the parlor of the girls' dormatory. I can just see Mary coming down that long stairway to the strains of 'Here Comes the Bride' if anyone uses that music these days."

An hour later Badger went to his bed and George stayed on the couch until morning.

CHAPTER XIII

EASTER SATURDAY MORNING

you are forever April
to me
the eternally unready,
                    "Song,"   William Carlos Williams

      Badger didn't remember having dreamed, but he woke with the joy of one who spent the night in reverie. He was in the bathroom shaving before he remembered that George had spent the night on the living room couch. He finished his ablutions and crossed the hall separating the two parts of his apartment, looked down at the couch and saw nothing but a sheet of lined notebook paper. He picked it up.

> Badger,
> Thanks for your hospitality. I'm sure you were preparing to serve me bacon and eggs with a side dish of fried potatoes but I just couldn't wait. I have retired to my palacial estate to "freshen up," as they say in the more sensationalistic Bohemian prose of the day. Don't give your nuptual plans a thought I will have made all the arrangements right away. All will be <u>sans souci</u>. My, but you certainly sleep late!
> > George

      Badger looked at his watch. Nine-sixteen. He rushed back to the bedroom, grabbed two socks of the same general shade, shorts and tee shirt. Picking slacks and shirt were a bit more difficult. He tried on a blue shirt but remembered he had worn a blue shirt on Thursday. He settled on a multi colored sport shirt, brownish slacks with glossy knees and equally glossy bottom. He picked up a wind breaker from the chair and headed out of the room, down the stairs and into his car. He had no time to waste. He knew what George would be doing. He would be telling every living soul on campus, and a few whose souls were not really active enough to be called living, about the engagement. And there was one thing that Badger perceived as the prerogative of the prospective groom and that was that he should be allowed to announce his own engagement to living and dead souls alike. Sans souci indeed! There was much to worry about, and John Badger Smith was a born worrier.

The trip up the Hill was fast, but not fast enough for a man with a mission. He parked his car in the library parking lot and walked at a trotter's pace to the Lion's Den, where he found his two aunts and Mary sipping coffee. All three had Cheshire grins that told Badger he was too late.

"Johnny, we approve. Your taste in fiancees is equal to your taste in great aunts," said Blanche.

"The date is perfect for us, the week-end of the twenty-ninth of May. The wedding on a Saturday," said Bernadine. "We are looking forward to it."

"I do think, Badger, that it would have been better if you had consulted me about the date of the wedding," said Mary in a tone of mild reproof. She glanced at the Badger sisters and smiled. "Nothing was said last night about when we would get married, but the week-end of the twenty-ninth will be just fine."

"The date and arrangements were not made by me. George was waiting last night when I got home. As soon as I told him we were engaged he took over. He chose the date and the place and. . . . ."

"You'll be married in the little church at the foot of the Hill won't you, Johnny?" asked Bernadine.

"We can't. The church will be undergoing major renovation at that time. George wants us to be married in the girl's dormatory."

"The girl's dormatory!" two altos and a soprano sang out in cacophonic counterpoint.

Before Badger could respond to this, a shadow covered the table part of the booth. All four looked up to see, not the attractive waitress standing with a coffee pot in her hand but Sgt. Reburg with his hands on his hips and a broad smile on his face.

"Why Chuck," said Bernadine, "pull up a chair and join us."

"Thank you, Bernadine. I will. I saw Professor Mercater a short time ago and he told me of the engagement. Congratulations, Badger and. . . I can never remember what it is that one is supposed to say to the lady."

"That's all right," said Mary. "I don't think many people can."

The sergeant picked up a chair from a nearby table and joined the group just in time for the attractive waitress to appear with two more mugs and a pot of coffee. She filled all the mugs with the black mud the Lion's Den was noted for, took orders for sweet rolls and left.

"A great deal has been happening since I saw you yesterday. For one thing, my immediate supervisor, a man whose mental ability to memorize the entire *Missouri State Police Code of Conduct* has left his brain capable of absolutely nothing else, has had a long talk with his supervisor and has, as a consequence, been promoted to a position where he has nothing to do with me. I have been notified that I am in complete charge of this case. This means I can conduct the investigation as I see fit. Also, according to a Mrs. or Miss or Ms Schmidt, besides getting engaged last night two young people at this very table also had time to have a look around Larry Sermons' room."

Both Bernadine and Blanche looked unhappy, Mary looked trapped, but Badger looked almost pleased as he sipped his coffee.

"As you know, Chuck, we found no books or other tangible evidence in the room," said Badger. "Mary and I did, however, notice that there were marks under the bed of dust that had been disrupted as if by a box or something being scraped along the floor."

"I wondered if you had noticed that, Badger. Very good! And, of course, some of the foot marks outside the window were yours," said Reburg.

Badger cringed slightly then looked at Mary. "I went back to the Schmidt house after I left you last night. I wanted to see if someone had climbed in Sermons' window. I couldn't tell." He looked back at Reburg. "I was outside the window when you were talking to Mrs. Schmidt. When did you see the outside?"

"I didn't. One of my men saw you. As long as my

ex-boss was in charge I couldn't investigate Sermons' room, but I could keep tabs on who went in and out of that house. My man reported that someone fitting your descriptions had entered the house. That was excuse enough for me to investigate. When I left, my man reported by phone that you had been outside the window. We had already investigated that area rather thoroughly by the way. I really believe that we could do much better if you and I were working together rather than as it was last night.."

"I agree," said Badger. "If your man saw Mary and me go up to the house and later saw me outside the window, then he must also have seen whoever it was that Mrs. Schmidt wouldn't let into the house and the one who climbed in the window."

We have zero on both counts. The window marks were made before yesterday morning when I put a man to watch the house and the boy who came up trying to get into Sermons' room got away from us. We have a good description of him but that's all. But he didn't get in."

The attractive coed had brought the sweet rolls and poured more coffee. In addition she had given Reburg both a big smile and the check.

"What is the situation now, as you see it, Chuck?" Bernadine asked.

"Well, first we have the theft and forgeries of the books. There are a number of details there that we don't understand. From what has been said at the meetings it would seem most likely that the books were taken to go into the collection of some connoisseur. He may have stolen the books himself, or paid someone to do it, or he might be involved knowingly or unknowingly after the fact."

"It seems to me," said Bernadine, "that it would not be after the fact or the thief wouldn't have known what books to steal."

"But remember, Bernadine," broke in Blanche, "that some of the books had no monitary or artistic value, as if they had been stolen by a person of very limited literary knowledge."

"Then there is the death, now quite clearly the murder, of Larry Sermons," continued Chuck Reburg, as if neither of the Badger sisters had spoken a word. "He was struck on the head with a weapon that we haven't found, and one I'm afraid we might never find. That he was discovered in the Archives, where all the book thefts occurred, leaves little doubt that the murder and thefts were related."

"That just makes common sense," said Mary.

"Next we have the shooting death of Jack Zinecor." Reburg continued without even noticing Mary's interuption. "That really does confuse everything. It occurred away from the Archives , and with a different method. That is highly unusual. Most murderers stay with the same general method. We've checked. No twenty-two's sold in town."

Badger broke in. "There might be an explanation if we consider that Larry Sermons' murder was not planned, that the murderer went to the Archives only to talk to Sermons. Or maybe he didn't know Sermons would be there and hit him to keep the man quiet. Hard to tell at this point. Murdering him left the situation open for who knows what? Blackmail, perhaps. On the other hand. The murder of Zinecor was obviously planned, at least to some extent. Having murdered once it was now easier for him to murder again, but this time it was all worked out. I often see twenty-two pistols advertised in cataloges."

"Professor Smith, there's a phone call for you." The attractive coed was standing at the table with her ever present coffee pot. "You can take it behind the counter."

"Thank you, Jessica." Badger excused himself and got up and went to the counter while the coed poured more coffee.

"I really believe that more attention should be placed on the particular books that were stolen," said Bernadine.

"I agree, Bernadine," said Reburg, "and since you ladies know a great deal more about books than I do, I would like you to give as much attention to the books as you can. Perhaps you can see some connection among the books that the rest of us have overlooked. I know I'm being a bit selfish. You three are here on vacation and tomorrow is Easter, and Mary here must have many thing to do to plan her wedding."

Blanche smiled at Mary then looked at Reburg. "I believe that we can give up a bit of our vacation for the good of the State of Missouri and Carlton-Stokes College, and the criminal justice system in general" she said. "And I'm sure that Mary will receive just as much help between now and the wedding as Bernadine and I are allowed to give. Am I correct, Bernadine?"

"Of course, Blanche. I think Mary understands that." Bernadine turned to Chuck Reburg. "Is there any particular proceedure you want us to follow, or do you just want us to think about the books?"

"Well, I believe that if you go over to the Archives and worked directly with Graham Carruth that the results would be better than if you just sat around and thought."

"I really don't believe I will finish my coffee," said Blanche. "If I do I will just float my way over to the library. The school could add considerably to its library acquisitions if that young lady could be persuaded to pour just a little less coffee each day."

The three woman scooted from the booth as one, in a manner reminiscent of a George Ballanchine ballet.

Sgt. Reburg stood up and moved his chair out of the way. "I will go with you to explain to Mr. Carruth why you are there. You have probably noted that he is sometimes a rather difficult person."

Badger hung up the wall phone behind the counter and walked back to the booth. "All ready to go, I see. Where is it we are going?"

Reburg placed the check on the booth table along with some crumpled up bills then took Bernadine by the elbow and led her to the door. "We are going to the library so that the ladies can do some work on the stolen books. After they get settled in I would like you to come with me, Badger. There are still a few things that need to be cleared up concerning your invasion of Larry Sermons room last night."

"Who called you, Badger? asked Mary. "Or is that a secret?"

"My friend George has been very busy this morning. That was Father McLaughlin. He is sure he can talk the bishop into allowing us to be married in the girl's dormatory, although he personally prefers marrying us in La Grange. We'll have to see Father this afternoon."

Mary squeezed Badger's hand. I certainly had no idea when we started out on our late night walk that today we would be planning our marriage less than two months away. I really believe that I should take a look at the girl's dormatory *before* we see Father."

"Chuck, Mary and I are going to take a slight detour to look at the parlor of the girl's dorm. We won't be long."

The five had left the building and were on the sidewalk that led to the library and the fork that would take Mary and Badger to the girl's dormatory. The two lovers passed the slow moving threesome and walked rapidly ahead. They turned at the fork and were soon at the steps to the dormatory. They entered the building where a cleaning crew was moving furnature, dusting, and washing windows.

"Oh, Badger, it's lovely!"

They stood just inside the doorway and looked up at the long stairway down which, George had previously decided, Mary would decend at the beginning of the ceremony. To their left was the parlor with plenty of room for chairs to be set up, and a grand piano faced out toward them. Best of all, there was a fireplace in front of which the two could be married. Mary was entranced. This was better than a church. Married on the campus of Badger's college!

Not long afterward , the two walked happily into the Archives to see Bernadine, Blanche, and Sgt. Reburg joined by a very tired Graham Carruth sitting at the table in an obviously agitated and animated state. Everyone was talking at once.

"What's the matter?" Badger's big bass voice sounded like General William Booth entering into Heaven.

"I've found another missing work," said Graham. "Not a book this time, but an original manuscript of a Mark Twain satiric letter that until last year hadn't even been published. We were keeping it here so that it could be studied by one of our professors. It isn't ours."

"Not 'The Question,' that work that Rick Solmes discovered!" said Badger.

CHAPTER XIV

LATE EASTER SATURDAY MORNING

In a pattern called a war
Christ! What are patterns for?,
"Patterns," Amy Lowell

"Perhaps someone should explain," said Bernadine. "We are not familiar with a work called 'The Question'."

Graham was very happy to accommodate. "Prof. Solmes is one of our most interesting faculty members. He is in the English department with Badger and has developed a special interest in Mark Twain. That interest and expertize persuaded the Board of Directors of the Samuel Clemens Museum to appoint him curator. He found the work while going through some old yellowed papers. The writing itself hasn't been lost, since Prof. Solmes published it in a newsletter called The Clemensian, a newsletter that he edits. But the original is missing! This will be very embarassing to Prof. Solmes and to the college and to me as well."

"Would it help if we knew something about the contents of the work?" asked Blanche. "What is it about? If you will excuse my ending with a preposition."

Graham Carruth looked at Badger and

nodded to him.

"It's a short piece," said Badger, written in the form of a letter, using the persona of a Russian czar. Certainly, it's not Twain at his best. It's bitter, as some of his late work was, but it's still Twain with his unmistakable humor. How'd you find it was missing, Graham? Where did you have it?"

"It was in a locked drawer of a cabinet in the next room, below the bookcase along with some other papers, one of which was a list of acquisitions in the Archives that I needed. When I unlocked the drawer I saw that everything was out of place and the Twain letter, which had been in a large, unmarked manilla envelope, was gone."

Badger started to get up from his chair but was stopped by Sgt. Reburg, who stepped behind him and put his hands on his shoulders.

"I don't think you have to look, Badger. I already checked the drawer. There were no marks on the lock. Whoever took the Twain piece had to have had a key. The lock wasn't forced."

"That's impossible. I'm the only one with a key to that drawer. No one could have gotten in there."

"But someone obviously did," said Reburg. "And since the lock wasn't forced, a key had to have been used."

Something flashed in Badger's brain. He had taught logic in composition class too long to let Reburg's statement stand. "Wait a minute, Chuck. You're stating it as if there were only two possibilities.

The simple term for that is an 'either or fallacy.' There could be other options. Graham, are you sure the manuscript was placed in the drawer?"

Graham looked almost insulted as he answered. "Professor Solmes and I placed the manuscript in the envelope together, placed it in the drawer and I closed it and locked it. It was definately in the drawer."

"That had to have been over a week ago, before Rick went on vacation. Haven't you opened the drawer since?" Badger asked.

"Only once. When we were looking for the missing books. I checked to see if the manuscript was there. It was."

"Were you alone?" Badger continued.

"No. As a matter of fact, all of my helpers and Dr. Lehr were with me. It was Jack Zinecor who held the envelope as I slipped the papers back in. Then he placed it in the drawer."

Badger stood up, again. "If you will all follow me into the next room, I think I can show you how the envelope disappeared from the drawer, and I'm sure I know who stole it."

The scraping of chair legs across the floor was enough to make any librarian wince, and it should be noted that Bernadine, Blanche, and Graham were certainly not just any librarians. The group moved into the next room with Badger in the lead and Sgt. Reburg only a few steps behind. Badger opened the cabinet door below the drawer then knelt down. Using a pencil, he reached his hand far into the cabinet and probed about. After a few minutes he grunted and pulled out a wrinkled white business envelope addressed to the Carlton-Stokes Library and handed it to Graham.

"Was this in the drawer, Graham?"

"Yes, but how?"

"But how did I get it out of the drawer? Every drawer I have ever seen of this type has at least a one or two inch gap between the back of the drawer and the back of the piece of furniture or the wall. This one has several inches. All one has to do is poke the eraser end of a pencil up in the gap and anything that is shooved all the way back can be forced out. That envelope was undoubtedly pushed way back by the larger envelope of the Twain manuscript that Jack Zinecor forced, just as I demonstrated."

"Hold on a minute!" said Sgt. Reburg. "How in the." He saw Bernadine out of the corner of his eye. "How in heck do you get Jack Zinecor in this and what gave you the idea that that's how the Twain manuscript was stolen?"

Bernadine and Blanche both smiled. They elicited the same behavior from many men.

"Don't worry, Chuck. Both Bernadine and I have heard the word 'hell' used in public before. I believe I even saw it once in print, in something Shakespeare wrote."

"For as long as I can remember I have been overloading my desk drawers to the point where they get caught and will not open. If you will be honest I'm sure you will admit to doing the same. If there is a drawer above it, the solution is very easy. Simply pull out the top drawer and remove whatever is stuck below it. If, however, it is a top drawer, then the solution is more difficult. That's how I know there is a gap. I have many times had a stuck drawer and had to pull out the lower drawer and work from there. If there was nothing towards the back it would sometimes take hours, but if some papers were way in the back then a pencil and a few minutes would do the trick. I knew it had to be Jack Zinecor because, as Graham said, he not only held the envelope but put it in the drawer. He would have put it in as far back as he could so that he could get it out as I have demonstrated."

"Excuse me, Mr. Carruth," Mary said softly , "I personally don't believe that you took the manuscript, but why couldn't it have been you who took it? All you had to do was take out your key and open up the drawer. Now, doesn't that seem the most logical solution, Badger?"

"Yes, it does, too logical or obvious. If he had taken it he would simply have kept his mouth shut until all of this was over and then have it out with Rick Solmes. No, if Graham were dishonest he would have taken the manuscript in a manner that would not have left him so out in the open."

"I can see that," said Mary, "That is really my point. No one would suspect Mr. Carruth for just the reason you have given."

"That is true. You have a very good point , Mary. The biggest problem, however, is motive. Let me ask you a question. How many books would you say are in my aunts' apartment in Oak Meadow?"

"Several hundred, I should say."

"Doesn't that strike you as a bit strange? Only several hundred books in the apartment of two avid readers and lovers of books?"

"Well, no. Bernadine and Blanche worked with books all day long and could check out any that they wanted. They still can since they do volunteer work with me in the St. Edward School library. They don't need to own books. They are around books all day long."

"My point exactly! Graham also is around books all day long. Some librarians have very large personal libraries. But many do not, especially those who are old enough to have suffered through those years when teachers and librarians were at the very bottom of the economic heap. Graham's only motive would be to sell the Twain manuscript. That would be fine, except that Graham has as much knowledge of trafficing in stolen books as Bernadine and Blanche have."

Graham gave Mary a snide glance then smiled at Badger as the group walked back into the main room and again sat down around the table.

"Back to my point," said Badger. "I believe that Jack Zinecor stole the Twain manuscript in the fashion I have described and then one of the following occured: Zinecor contacted Mr. X and arranged to meet him, with the intention of selling the article. Mr. X preferred getting the work free and killed Zinecor. OR Mr. X saw Zinecor steal or deduced that Zinecor stole the article and killed him for it. There is one other possibility: Zinecor might have known who Larry

Sermons' murderer was and was murdered himself to keep everything quiet."

"How could Mr. Zinecor uncover who killed Larry Sermons if we haven't been able to figure it out?" asked Bernadine.

"He could very well be privy to some information that we know nothing about," said Reburg. "The four collectors knew each other and each other's special interests and methods."

After a lull in the conversation, Bernadine looked around the room, smiled at Mary and said, "Perhaps we should get back to our discussion of the missing books." There was a general assent and she continued. "So that I don't forget, I believe I will write down the names of all of the missing works." She pulled a pen and note pad from her purse and wrote as she talked. "First there is *The Scarlet Letter.* What year, Badger?"

Bernadine knew the date as well as any Hawthorne scholar, but she wanted to give Badger the floor and allow him to remain in charge.

"That was 1850, Bernadine. *Wieland* was 1798, I believe," said Badger, smiling and answering his aunt.

"Yes, and, a, Cooper's *The Spy* was 1821," broke in Graham Carruth, who wished to have some of the dubious glory of knowing the date of a particular work.

"Do I get a prize," said Blanche, "for remembering that *The History of the Town of Plymouth* was 1835?"

Graham looked irritated and Badger once again smiled.

"None of the other books have dates that really matter, except perhaps Kate Chopin's. *The Awakening* is in the last century, but just barely," said Blanche, "1899. All of the rest are twentieth century."

While she was talking the door opened and Edmund Linehan and Coral Reiser entered quietly and took seats, Coral sitting next to Graham, where Doug Boito had sat previously.

"Glad you two could come," said Reburg. "We were just going over everything we know, a bit of a refresher. Are any of the other committee members going to join us?"

"I think they'll all be here in a moment," said Edmund Linehan. They were coming down from the parking lot just as we entered the building, everyone except George."

"Oh, I believe I saw George wandering over the campus a short time ago, looking like a love sick puppy. I'm sure he will be finding his way into the Archives soon enough." Coral looked around the room and smiled.

The door opened again and the room was filled with the rest of the Archives committee, sans George Mercater, but the members had barely seated themselves when George burst through the door.

"Ah, I see I am the last to arrive, unless, of course, you are expecting your three closest friends, Graham." George gave Graham the nastiest look he could muster and sat down in his place, leaving a gap of several chairs between him and Coral, whom he snubbed.

Sgt. Reburg took back the floor and filled the new members in on the latest missing work and Badger's deductions, totally ignoring Graham's attempts to interupt him. After many questions and very few answers Badger was asked by Bernadine to present all that he knew and all that he surmised had happened. Badger cleared his throat in a nervous gesture.

"I've given most of my theories to a number of you many times in the last few days, but I'll try once again as the Bard says to be: 'Seeking the bubble reputation / Even in the cannon's mouth.' "

Graham Carruth leaned over to Coral Reiser. "Must that ham forever be quoting somebody or other?"

"First of all, I believe that Larry Sermons was contacted to steal *The Scarlet Letter* from the Archives and replace it with the forged second edition. Since the theft went so well, he had Sermons steal *Wieland, The Spy,* and *The History of the Town of Plymouth* but in what order I don't know. But because forgery of *The Scarlet Letter* was done with great care and expense, it is obvious it was the first. At this point Sermons realized that there was something special in these books, special enough for someone to pay him adequate money to buy a good used car down at Berry and Jack's filling station. With this thought he stole the other books, not books of great value, for he had no idea of the worth of books, but volumes that appeared expensive because they had fancy covers and illustrations, these he could easily pick out without someone telling him where they were on the shelves."

"And he then tried to sell them to the forger," said Dr. Lehr.

"Maybe," said Badger, "but I doubt it. I don't believe that the forger was aware of the theft of *The People, Yes* until after Graham made the discovery of its disappearance. Sermons probably thought he could sell the books easily. He wasn't very bright, but he did have enough street smarts to know that the forger would be unhappy with the extra thefts. I think he might have tried to sell them to one of Graham's book collector friends."

"Of course," broke in Onorio Flores. "He sold them to Jack Zinecor and the forger killed Zinecor for the books."

"I don't think so, Charlie," said Badger. "Both Zinecor and Gary Jurgenson are, or were, from out of town. It is very unlikely that Sermons knew either one of them too well. I'm sure, however, that he did know or know of James Craig and Dennis Marlin. They were both on campus quite regularly, and Craig's mansion would be difficult not to notice. It is possible he contacted one of them or intended to."

"It sounds as if you are dismissing them as suspects," said Bernadine. "I would think they were the prime suspects."

A cacophony of responces filled the room. "So would I." "You can't count those two out!" "Oh, come on, Badger!"

"Wait one moment, Mr. Smith," broke in Dr. Lehr. "If Marlin and Craig are innocent that pretty well leaves Jurgenson or one of us as the killer. I doubt very much that one of the good, people of Walden would have enough interest in rare books to steal and murder."

"No, no, no!" Badger almost yelled. "I'm not dismissing anyone. We don't even know if Sermons was contacted *directly* by the forger or if he knew the party. I'm simply saying that it isn't likely that he contacted Jurgenson or Zinecor. He may not have known them, but they might have known of him, if what Aunt Kate said about him was true. Also, almost any one of the faculty could have committed the crime. One of those not here in the room or even one of the faculty who apparently left the campus and Walden on this vacation could have returned or never left at all."

Mary reached out her right hand and squeezed Badger's left. "Perhaps you should go ahead quickly before there is mutiny on the *H. M. S. Archives.*"

"Right, Mary." Badger again cleared his throat. "I think the forger paid Sermons to steal the books, became furious when his forgeries were uncovered because of Sermons' stupid thefts and killed him. In an unrelated incident Zinecor took 'The Question,' as I demonstrated, but was murdered by someone, probably the forger, either to obtain Twain's manuscript or to keep Zinecor quiet for some unknown reason."

"There seem to be holes in your story," said Dr.Lehr. "I don't think we're close to solving the case."

"Maybe closer than you think, Doctor."

❦   ❦   ❦

CHAPTER XV

EASTER SATURDAY NIGHT AND MORNING

1 cannot find my way: there is no star
In all the shrouded heavens anywhere.
         "Credo,"   Edwin Arlington Robinson

Dinner was not what it had been the previous two nights. George had not returned to Badger's apartment but had gone tagging after Coral and Graham. With George missing and with Badger's cupboard almost bare the group had walked over to Aunt Kate's after cocktails and

> They dined on mince, and slices of quince,
> Which they ate with a runcible spoon.

The rain of the night before threatened to return. Clouds filled the sky while the four sipped brandy and coffee in Badger's small apartment, partly in an attempt to neutralize Aunt Kate's greasy steaks and fries.

"Johnny, there are many, many mysteries in our world," began Bernadine, "but the greatest of these is how you can keep a home almost totally void of groceries and yet always have plenty of coffee and brandy.

"One should always take care of the necessities first," said Badger, "and if the necessities are also the rhapsodies, so much the better."

"I agree," said Mary. "We should be spending this evening discussing the necessities and rhapsodies of our coming nuptuals."

Bernadine and Blanche were quick to assent, so the remainder of the evening was spent, not in discussing murder and vice and everything nice, but in discussing and planning the wedding of Mary (nee) Cronin Mallony and John Badger Smith. It was past eleven when Badger escorted the three ladies back up to the campus in Mary's car, kissed his aunts good night, and walked Mary back out where he planned they could gaze at the stars. The stars, however, had no intention of revealing themselves to the lowly mortals and hid themselves behind the midwest's only mountains. The two walked over to the brink of the Hill and looked down on the town. All they could see was the church directly below them and a few dim lights beyond. After that all was dark. Walden was engulfed in fog.

"I don't remember seeing any fog when we drove up here, and that was only a few minutes ago," said Mary. "You may have trouble finding your way back home."

"When the fog steps in off the river it is not always on little cat feet. It sometimes is more like Gulliver walking in Lilliput. I'll keep my eyes wide open through the fog, just like a postman," said Badger, as he pulled Mary to him and kissed her as if he were leaving her for months rather than for a few hours.

The lovers walked quietly hand in hand back to Lueker Hall until Mary broke the silence. "I realize that you would have preferred spending the evening talking about the murders, but I'm glad we were able to settle so many of the plans for the wedding. It was good to have Bernadine and Blanche to help us. They can be very practical without being stodgy."

"I didn't mind at all not talking about the murders, first because we have been saying the same things over and over and secondly, the subject palls before the thought of out marriage and life together."

Mary stopped and put her arms around Badger's neck. "Oh, Johnny, I do love you. You don't mind if I call you Johnny, do you? Occasionally? When we're alone."

"When we're alone."

Badger kissed his fiancee, walked with her into Lueker Hall, turned, and walked back to the edge of the Hill and started down the steps into the fog below, which was not nearly so dense as the fog in his head. He reached the bottom by the church and could see a dim light coming from the rectory next door. Father McLaughlin must still be awake. Badger climbed the two steps to the front door, stumbling on the second one and made enough noise to make ringing the bell superfluous. Father McLaughlin, pipe in mouth, was standing in the doorway when Badger looked up.

"Only you, Badger, would announce your arrival at midnight in such a manner. Come in! I'll see if I have any brandy to celebrate this milepost."

He held the door open and Badger walked into the small but comfortable living room and sat down in one of the two chairs, the one that did not have a book lying open on the seat. He looked around as Father McLaughlin went into the kitchen. Most of the wall space was taken up with bookcases filled with novels, collections of poetry and essays and various religious tracts. A large photograph over the mantle of a bishop was signed. Father McLaughlin returned with a tray with two brandy snifters generously filled. He placed the tray on a table between the two chairs while Badger lifted the book.

"Been re-reading *Lady Chatterly*, Father?"

Father McLaughlin turned the book over to show the title. "No, but something just as prurient, *The Scarlet Letter*. That Nathaniel Hawthorne was certainly lascivious! Why here at the beginning is a tale of a young lady who is with child. There is no telling what I am apt to find if I should read further."

"Jack, you are a strange one. Sitting up at midnight on Easter morning reading Hawthorne when in a few hours you have to say mass and deliver your most important sermon of the year."

"I really thought I should refresh myself on *The Scarlet Letter* in view of what has happened up the Hill. I haven't read it since I was in high school. As for my sermon, that is no problem at all. I will use the same one I delivered last year. Since everyone slept through it then, it will sound new and fresh to those few who stay awake in the morning." The two friends laughed and Father Jack , as many of his parishoners called him, lifted his snifter.

"A toast to my friend who is going to the alter once more."

"Sorry that Mary and I didn't get down to see you this afternoon. Our mystery just keeps getting deeper and deeper. You know, of course, that it was George who picked the time and place."

"I will have to contact the bishop. I'll let you know what he has to say. He will, of course, suggest you marry in La Grange, but I think I can talk him into the dorm idea, maybe on the basis of size. My La Grange church is rather small, and I assume there'll be quite a large crowd. The bishop gives in to me often, mainly because I have two churches. For example, I have never approved of midnight masses for this community, too many problems. The bishop leaves me alone on that issue. He knows I'm just an old fashoned boy!"

Before the snifters were empty the two men had discussed the wedding in detail, made arrangements for Father Jack to meet Mary after mass, settled the major problems of the world, and had returned to *The Scarlet Letter*.

"I find Hawthorne's portrayal of Dimmesdale particularly interesting. The clergy are most often presented in our fiction as sanctimonious literalists with no faults at all. It is rather easy to avoid sin if you are never tempted." Father Jack was off and running on one of his favorite subjects. "The Brittish, on the other hand, are more apt to humanize their clergy. Take W. Somerset Maugham. His 'Rain' depicts a human, even though vicious member of the cloth."

At any other time, this conversation on literature might have gone on until the brandy bottle in the kitchen was empty, but on this particular occasion Father Jack needed to have his curiosity fed. Like everyone else in Walden he was absorbed in the book thefts and the murders of two men right on campus.

After being filled in on all the details Father Jack set down his empty snifter, relit his full pipe and looked at Badger.

"It is very interesting how those men were brought in by your librarian to search out the library and the Archives. You said they weren't being paid. I wonder why they are doing it? The answer to that might tell us a great deal about this whole affair, don't you think?"

Badger stood and moved towards the door. He was aware that Father John needed his sleep so as to be ready to deliver the homily he had finished, not the year before, but just fifteen minutes before Badger had arrived, and Badger needed to retrieve thoughts of Mary and all that that involved.

After a short farewell, the two parted, for, without question, the greatest difference between the genders besides the unequivocal is the time it takes to say good-bye. Badger walked down the street with no difficulty in finding his way. The fog had lifted from both the atmosphere and the brain. His mind was clear. He wasn't quite sure what it was that he thought, but he knew that there were some very important ideas solidly inbedded in his brain which would rise when they were needed.

The fog had lifted, but the night was still starless yet filled with the romance of rumbling thunder far in the distance. Badger flicked on the hall light and checked his watch while he climbed the stairs to his apartment. One thirty-five. Plenty of time to lie in bed and stare into the darkness and think about Mary.

*   *   *

One of nature's many jokes is that a good night's sleep is always granted to those who need it the least. Badger was asleep seconds after he closed his eyes and he did not open them again until his alarm clock radio told him that the clouds and rain of the past few days would continue on this Easter morn.

Badger performed his ablutions and dressed in a tan suit and soft brown shoes. He was almost out the door when he remembered what the radio voice had told him, pulled open the shade to his single bedroom window, peered out on the wet morning, and changed into a dark blue suit and black shoes. The idea of a raincoat could not enter his mind, which was too filled with more important and exciting matter.

When he reached the campus he pulled his car around to the side of Lueker Hall and found the three ladies waiting for him by the desk, void of a clerk. He kissed all three with some difficulty, as they all wore broad brimmed hats.

"I'm afraid we will have to forego any breakfast," said Blanche. "The Lion's Den appears to be closed this Easter morn."

"I don't mind passing up breakfast," said Bernadine, "I like the old fashioned fasting before receiving communion. But I do miss not having a cup of coffee."

Badger looked at his watch. "We have plenty of time to drive down to Aunt Kate's for coffee before mass. Coffee is all that I can recommend. Kate's Sunday cook is worse than her regular one and has trouble with cold cerial, much less eggs."

Aunt Kate's was indeed open and doing a thriving business. Because they arrived without the siren blowing they were not met at the door and not escorted to the booth that had just been vacated. A surly young man cleared their table and left four dripping glasses of water. Then walked back behind the counter before anyone had a chance to ask for coffee.

" 'I'm apt to be surly / Getting up early'," quoted Blanche.

A woman sitting at a table with three other women got up and came over to the booth. "Prof. Smith." It was Beverly Schmidt. "If you look over at the counter. The boy who's just paying is the one that came to my house the other night ."

All four looked and watched as the boy walked quickly out of the cafe. "Thank you Mrs. Schmidt," said Badger and Mary in unison as Mrs. Schmidt made her way back to her companions and Aunt Kate, like the battleship *Missouri* , approached the table.

"Regular or decaf?"

"Kate, do you know who that boy was who just paid and left?" Mary was starting to feel at home in Walden and wasn't afraid to take over part of the interrogation.

"That, Honey, is Tommy Thorson, lives just north of town on 61. Works as a farm hand when someone will hire him," answered Kate, as she poured the designated coffee. "Why?"

"Oh, nothing. It's just that he looks exactly like

someone up near Chicago. Thought maybe it was a brother or something, but a different last name."

"No, couldn't be. All Tommy's relatives are from down around Memphis, where I come from. Want something besides coffee this morning?" Four heads shook no and Kate walked away. "If you want anything just let me know."

"Mary Mallony! Such fabrication!" Exclaimed Blanche. "And on Easter Sunday! I couldn't have done better myself."

"That information should help Chuck to get a few more facts," said Badger.

"So it's back to Chuck," said Bernadine, sipping her coffee. "I'm glad that he is now in complete charge of the investigation. You know, if this Tommy Thorson was hired by the killer to take something from Larry Sermons' apartment then we might just have the murderer in jail before this day is through. Listen to me, 'we might just have,' as if Blanche and I had anything to do with it."

"Chuck said yesterday that he would be at the church before mass to give us an update. Mary can give her report then."

"The four drank their coffee and observed the comings and goings of the people of Walden through the portals of Aunt Kate's until it was time to head for the church. Bernadine insisted on paying the check and the four walked to the car and were in front of the church in just a few minutes. Father Jack pulled into his parking spot on his way back from saying mass in La Grange. Badger had to let the ladies out, make a u-turn, park half way down the block, and walk back, which he did in a matter of minutes. When he approached the church he could see Chuck Reburg talking to Mary and his aunts.

"I see you have these three working for you, Badger," said the sergeant by way of a greeting. "I guess I had better get after this Tommy Thorson and see what I can find out. See you all later."

The three watched Chuck Reburg stretch his legs down the sidewalk to his squad car and drive off as if he had nothing to do.

"I think we had better go in while there is still a place for us," said Bernadine, and led the way into the little church, which was void of stained glass windows, save one above the alter, and the marble icons that adorn her big city cousins, but it was filled with a subdued dignity, nevertheless. A children's choir occupied the first two rows on the Blessed Virgin side of the church, and as so often happens in many churches of all denominations, the two front rows on the other, or St Joseph side, were unoccupied, so the valiant pilgrims sat, stood, and knelt in the front row.

Father Jack came down the aisle behind his alter boys and the two lay readers, to the tune of "Holy God, We Praise Thy Name." Father John McLaughlin was indeed an old fashioned priest, even though he had converted a Benediction hymn into a Processional psalm. He stepped into the sanctuary and mass began. The lay readers gave Father Jack time to collect his thoughts. After another hymn and a number of prayers and the reading of the Epistle and Gospel Father Jack began his homily which ended:

"As my old parish priest, Mgr. John Code, wrote many years ago, 'As valiant Christian warriors let us follow in the footsteps of the Crucified, and the grave will be for us no longer a house of horrors, nor an abode of darkness. It will be instead a peaceful sepulchre, a sleeping place, a station of transfer whence with radiant spirit we pass heavenward with the Angel of the Resurrection.'"

As was not unusual, Badger Smith was in a reverie all his own, a reverie of a much earlier time and distant place. And, as memories invariably did, it brought up one of his poems and he recited almost out loud as Father Jack returned to the alter:

> Dust is a memory
> left too long
> in darkened places
> half gone wrong.
>
> Tears are reactions
> to dusty eyes
> from a stirred up past
> that never dies.

CHAPTER XVI

EASTER MORNING

In your Easter bonnet
With all the frills upon it
You'll be the finest lady
In the Easter Parade.
> *"Easter Parade," Irving Berlin*

When the Recessional ended and Father Jack was in the rear of the church, shaking hands with each of his parishoners as he left the church, Badger exited his front row seat and escorted his harem slowly to the back of the church. They were the last to leave since they were too slow in getting up to follow the ushers' directions.

"So, this is the young lady brave enough to take on a life with my friend Badger." Father Jack needed no introduction to get him started.

"Jack, as you surmissed, this is my fiancee, Mary Mallony, and my two great aunts, Bernadine and Blanche Badger." Then Badger turned to his two aunts and Mary. "And this is, of course, Father John McLaughlin, or Jack."

"I believe Badger and I ironed out all the wrinkles in your May wedding. So if someone can solve the double murder then it should be a lovely wedding. I saw you talking to the State Trooper before mass. Anything new?"

After explaining the Tommy Thorson episode and passing a few niceties, they all agreed to meet Father Jack at Coral Reiser's performance of *The Creation* that evening. When they stepped out of the church and saw that the clouds had dissipated to a few cumulo-cirrus, the sun was out and the day beautiful, Badger's offer to bring the car was laughed off and the three went arm in arm in arm down the narrow sidewalk toward the car, humming "Easter Parade." Just behind them came Badger, singing loudly Berlin's original lyric to the tune, "Smile and show your dimple / You'll find it very simple."

Once settled in the car with Blanche and Mary in the back and Bernadine with Badger in the front seat, Bernadine turned to her left. "Happy you are supposed to be, but why so giddy?"

Badger smiled and said slowly in a clear voice, "Last night without knowing it Jack helped me uncover the murderer.

"Johnny!" "Johnny!" "Who is it, Badger!" "Tell us. How do you know?" "Is it James Craig? I thought so all along." "Tell us, Johnny."

"I can't say right now. I need more proof."

Badger started the car and pulled into the driving lane. He was enjoying himself immensely. His three companions were far more giddy than he had been.

"I know who did it and how and why, but I can't prove it. I don't think there is any possibility of any further violence so there is no problem there. What Chuck Reburg finds out may solve the whole thing, but if it doesn't I still have my case, but how to prove it, how to prove it?

"Well, tell us who it is you suspect and we can help you," pleaded Mary.

"I would love to tell you everything, but in that case there would be a very good chance of violence, and I'm sure none of us wants that. Besides, I want a chance to clear up a few of the details."

The thunderous sounds of the three sulking women remaining absolutely silent in a closed car is enough to burst the ear drums and make any man give in, but Badger was not just any man.

There was a time in the history of man, even Twentieth Century man when keeping holy the Sabbath meant diners and grocery stores were closed. This was in a less enlightened age before Cole Porter wrote "Anything Goes." Badger pulled his car into the parking lot of the Remorg Shopping Center with it's motto on the overhead sign: "We Never Close." And Badger said out loud: "We have no key, / and there ain't no lock. / So we'll sell you bread / Around the clock."

The four entered the store where Bernadine took over. Blanche pushed the cart and Bernadine reached from shelf to shelf filling that cart with goods that would soon fill Badger's cabinets and refrigerator.

"We should get back just in time to fix a respectable lunch for the four of us. Make that five."

From a side aisle stepped a smiling George Mercater, who was pushing a cart ladened with groceries followed by Coral Reiser also smiling. They had the required one in three carts with an out of skew front wheel so they slid along.

"Better make that six, Bernadine," said Blanche.

"What a nice surprise!" said Coral. "George and I were just wondering if you were out of church yet. We've been out twenty minutes."

"We drove here straight from the service and were picking up a few things for lunch," said Bernadine. "Why don't you come and join us?"

"We would love to," said Coral.

"It looks to me like you were preparing for the world's greatest famine," said George. "We have a few more things to pick up, then need to take them back to Coral's place. We could be there in about an hour."

Coral put her hand over George's, which rested on the cart handle, and gave it a light squeeze. "Tell them what you asked me, George."

"Well," began George, "I asked Coral if . . . . ."

"Tell them, George!"

"I asked Coral if she would marry me."

"Tell them what I said, George."

"She said that she would."

After many " How wonderfuls," "Congratulations," kisses, hugs, and slaps on the back the six were subjected to a number of stares. They broke up, finished their shopping and left, Coral and George driving off in one car while Badger and his guests drove off in the Taurus.

"Well, that mystery is solved," said Mary.

"What mystery is that?" asked Blanche.

"I think she is referring to the mystery of why Coral accepted a date to go out to dinner with Graham Carruth," said Badger.

"That's right," said Mary.

"And why did she?" asked Bernadine.

"To make George jealous," said Mary.

Badger drove with one eye on the road and the other on the rear view mirror, so he could see the expressions in the back seat. "You may remember that I told you that George has been interested in several ladies in the time I have known him. George's interest always diminished as the young lady's increased."

"Coral seems to understand men very well," said Mary. "When we were at the check out she pulled me aside and said that the only reason she went out with Graham was to make George jealous, and it worked. She said that George followed her and Graham around last night until Graham became so angry that he went home. Then, this morning before church, George 'popped the question' as she said."

"With a little help from Coral," said Badger.

"Don't you realize by now, Badger, that it always takes two for a successful proposal," said Mary.

"If Coral was and is interested in George, and George is so obviously interested in Coral," began Bernadine, "then why in the name of Heaven would Graham Carruth ask Coral out on a date? It seems like a very nasty thing to do to one of your colleagues."

"That is certainly one of the questions that requires an answer, but I'm sure has nothing to do with the thefts and murders," said Badger.

When they reached Badger's apartment and the Taurus was parked, Blanche took Bernadine's arm and helped her up the stairs. Badger took two grocery bags and Mary took one and they followed the sisters. Bernadine's puffing was as nothing when compared to Badger's.

The groceries were put away, everyone used the facilities, Badger changed and the ladies converted their clothing so that it was a good deal more casual, and Badger had been summoned to the phone to answer a call from Jonathan Hayes, who informed him that he would not be returning to the school for another week. Badger felt it kinder not to mention the problems on campus to the president at this time so lied when asked if all was going well. After he thanked Eva for calling him to the phone and clearing up a few items with Victor, including borrowing as much ice as was in the Gibson household, he climbed back up the steps to his own apartment where Bernadine was preparing a lunch of cold salads, slices of corned beef, cheddar cheese, roast beef and bread. Blanche had made a large pitcher of sun tea which she had set by the south window on one of the kitchen chairs. She was now setting silverware and plates on the table in buffet style. Mary was sitting a bit uncomfortably on the couch in the living room.

"I have been delegated to this area to read or think or whatever I wish just so long as I do not get in the way of your two aunts."

Blanche took the ice bucket from Badger and returned to the kitchen where she placed it in the refrigerator, leaving the two in semi-private in the living room.

"What do you think about Bernadine's question?" asked Mary.

Badger took his pack of cigarettes from his shirt pocket, picked out a single with thumb and forefinger, placed it in his mouth and was about to light it, then took it back out of his mouth. "I don't think smoking is an addiction as everyone is trying to prove; I think it's a habit. And I assert I can control my penchants." He put the cigarette back in the pack and sat down next to Mary.

"What was your question, again?"

"Why do you think Graham asked Coral to dinner?" It really wasn't a very nice thing to do, and with his preoccupation with the thefts it seems to me a very strange behavior."

"It certainly does," called Bernadine from the kitchen.

Badger sat back on the couch, stretched his left arm so that it went around Mary's shoulder, cleared his throat and began talking as if he were lecturing a composition class on split infinitives.

"There are a number of reasons he might ask

Coral out. The first would be that he needed someone to talk to about the thefts and she was available. The second, or maybe it is really the first, is that he has a genuine affection for Coral and somehow saw a chance to take her away from George. Prissy and getting older though he may be, Graham is a man with the desires of a man."

Bernadine walked around the bookcase into the living room. She felt as though she should raise her hand before speaking. "What happened to the theory we had earlier that he may have been trying to get information from her?"

"The best way to check on that theory is to ask Coral what they talked about over dinner," said Badger. "However, I can't imagine what Coral might have known that everyone else didn't know or what Graham thought she might know."

Blanche called from the kitchen. "I think we may be putting too much significance on Graham Carruth's romantic life."

The sound of the lower door opening and closing below announced the arrival of Coral and George, which was confirmed by the sounds of footsteps on the stairs and the appearance of the newly engaged couple in the doorway.

After the greetings and after everyone was settled in the living room in the usual places plus an extra kitchen chair for Coral, who enjoyed a straight chair so that she sat higher than anyone else, Badger proceeded to make and serve Shannon County cocktails. For Coral this was something new and she was informed that this drink was orange juice and bourbon, a decided improvement over the more popular orange juice and vodka consumed by the masses.

"We don't wish to bring up a painful subject on this happy day," began Blanche, "but we were all wondering what it was that Coral and Graham Carruth were discussing over dinner the other night."

"Don't feel bad about it, Blanche," said George. "Coral and I will be laughing about that night for a good many years. Tell them, Honey."

"It is really strange," said Coral, "but we talked about nothing but music all night long. Every time I tried to change the subject to the lost books, Graham would act as though he hadn't heard me and continue to talk music. He has quite a knowledge of choral music of the Baroque period."

"Didn't he mention the missing books at all?" asked Mary.

"About the tenth time I mentioned them he said that he didn't want to talk or think about them. He said he wanted the evening to be a complete escape from his problems."

"That seems a valid response," said Badger. "Or a valid response for almost anyone but Graham Carruth. All of you saw the way he behaved at everyone of our meetings. He is so involved in his library that he thinks of nothing else and to spend an entire evening avoiding the subject seems quite strange. I think there is one more possible reason for the unusual date offer, besides, of course, your considerable charms, Coral."

Everyone was looking at Badger and no one was touching his drink, of course, except Badger, who was thoroughly enjoying his "Life upon the Wicked Stage" and the dramatic impact he was having.

"Graham might not have wanted to be alone that night," After he deemed a sufficient period of quiet had passed. If he had stayed at home he would surely have had at least one visitor, and maybe one whose questions Graham preferred not to answer." Coral smiled at this.

"There is one other possibility, but I'll let you all figure that one out for yourselves in your own time," said Coral.

The silence in the room called for one thing and one thing only. Bernadine made the announcement:

"Lunch is served."

CHAPTER XVII

EASTER NOON

> Keep us here
> All simply in the springing of the year.
> "A Prayer in Spring," Robert Frost

Lunch was a complete success. All the salads added to the zest of the sandwiches everyone made from the bread, meat and cheese. Blanche's sun tea had just enough time to steep, and the ice which Badger brought up from the Gibson's and for which his aunts praised him profusely, gave the tea a refreshing coolness. Left over chocolate cake finished off the repast perfectly.

Shortly after everyone had finished eating, Badger heard Eva calling from down stairs, "Telephone Badger!" He bounded out the door and took the steps two at a time. In about ten minutes he trudged up the steps and plopped down in the straight chair Coral had earlier vacated for a spot on the couch.

"That was Chuck Reburg. He located Tommy Thorson and took him to the Walden jail for interrogation. The boy says that first of all, he never got into Larry Sermons' room. He says he tried, but the rain at the time made the siding much too slippery for him to try to scale the wall and get into the window.

Chuck says the boy is rather puny for a farmer. Turns out his folks have a chicken ranch which doesn't require very powerful arms or much work from him. That's why he's hired out, as Aunt Kate told us. Chuck says he believes Tommy told the truth."

"Did he say who hired him to try to get into Sermons' room?" asked George, who, along with Coral, had been briefed on current events while they ate lunch.

"Sort of. He gave a description. This one shows how wrong I can be. It sounds just like Jack Zinecor hired him. He said this man approached him outside of Aunt Kate's and told him some books he had loaned were in Sermons' room. He didn't want to go their because some of the books were racy and was embarrassed to see the landlady. The man offered him ten bucks for the lot. He got five in advance."

While everyone was digesting the information, Badger once again was called to the phone. He returned this time taking two steps at a time but wearing a somewhat puzzeled look on his face.

"Chuck again. He just finished talking to the Quincy police. They searched Jack Zinecor's home and found some of the missing books." He took out a piece of paper and read. "*Mattias at the Door, The Hill, The People, Yes, Life and Morals of Jesus of Nazareth*, and *The Awakening*, all in a cardboard box. In his desk they found 'The Question'. This means Zinecor hired Thorson as a red herring."

Coral had to leave to go to the Church of the Redemption to run through a few of the numbers with the orchestra. The choir members were all supposed to be at home resting their voices. George drove her but promised to return in time for a dinner of Easter baked ham, *au graten* potatoes, out of a box, canned beans, and lettuce salad. Bernadine was not in the habit of using prepared or canned foods for special meals, but given the limited time and facilities she was happy for the convenience foods.

Once Coral and George had left everyone became very busy. Bernadine began preparing dinner, Blanche and Mary cleaned up after the mess made by six people eating a buffet lunch in crowded quarters, and Badger, like Miniver Cheevy, "rested from his labors." The new information did not sway Badger from his basic theory, but it did require that he answer for himself some new questions. So he lay on the couch, stared at the ceiling, and again like Miniver Cheevy, Badger "thought and thought and thought about it."

Before dinner, Badger had to drive the three ladies back to Lueker Hall so that they could change into clothes they felt were suitable for evening wear and a church concert. They returned to the apartment in plenty of time to finish their work on the dinner, fix cocktails and greet George when he arrived.

The cocktails and dinner were festive and delicious. Everyone had two helpings of ham, even though it had been carved by the inept hands of one John Badger Smith. The conversation remained light and humorous until Mary suggested that Coral and George make the May date into a double wedding. Everyone liked the idea until George remembered that Coral had a family somewhere around Elgin, Illinois.

Coffee was put off for the time being as George

had to get to the church on time to usher, and the rest wanted to get good seats. They walked slowly down the stairs and to the cars and then moved quickly to the church, which was only a few blocks away, a condition not unusual in Walden.

Badger let the ladies off in front of the church then found a parking spot a short distance away. Other cars were filling up the available parking space in a hurry and the sidewalks in all directions had people approaching the church aided by porch lights all on.

The Church of Redemption was the newest and largest church in Walden. It had the best organ and the best acoustics of any of its churches. The doors were flung wide open, for it was too early in the season for the mosquitoes and yellow jackets that plagued the town later in the season. A yellow light flooded out the doorway and multi-colored light oozed from the stained glass windows. The entry was crowded with people waiting to be ushered to their seats by George and two other men.

Badger looked about and saw Mary and his aunts waiting by the center aisle where George was ushering. Scanning the church he saw many people he knew including almost everyone on the Archives committee and a number of faculty members who had been out of town over the vacation. That none of them was required to be back before classes resumed on Tuesday morning attested to the considerable enticement of one Coral Reiser. He nodded to Eva and Victor Gibson, who were standing with friends against one wall.

"I'll put you about midway down," said George as he held out his arm to Bernadine. "You'll be able to see and hear everything perfectly." Blanche and Mary followed, and Badger quickened his pace so as to catch up. Once seated, the four had an opportunity to observe the congregation. Because the small orchestra was warming up and was making a considerable clamor no one felt compelled to observe the decorum of a church, so there was considerable din as well from the audience, adding to that of the musical instruments.

Mary looked at Badger. "Isn't this the church of Dr. Lehr?"

Badger nodded. "My guess is that he is up with Coral and the choir, wherever that is. He may make a little, or not so little, speech before the concert gets underway."

Before long the church was filled and the congregation quieted down. The orchestra stopped warming up and sat expectantly. A few stragglers found seats in less desirable places, and everyone stared at a door stage right which opened and Dr. Lehr entered and walked, cane in hand, to the portable lectern at the center of the sanctuary.

"Good evening," There was a low mumbling of returned 'Good evenings' from the congregation. "For those who have not been here before, I am Dr. Lehr, Pastor of the Church of the Redemption here in Walden. I welcome you all . . . . ."

Ten minutes later he was still orating while everyone, save one, was listened. Badger was enjoying the ornate carvings in the pillars on each side of the sanctuary. When he finally returned his attention to the lectern, Dr. Lehr was finishing up:

"Why talk of beauty? What could be more beautiful than these musicians and singers who have sacrificed their free time to rehearse this glorious music....."

Badger had once more lost contact with the dais and was reveling in thoughts of the Fourth of July and e. e. cummings' "next to of course god," which sounded a great deal like Dr. Lehr's sermon, and so missed the end of the speech, the entrance of the concert master followed by the tuning to the oboe A. He returned his attention when the choir entered, the ladies in dark blue or black skirts and white blouses and the men in dark slacks, white shirts and black ties followed by Coral Reiser in a flaming red dress, who then bowed while two young boys turned the lectern around to become her podium. She raised her baton and the concert began.

There are almost as many ways to conduct a musical group as there are conductors. Some, especially choir and choral directors, prefer to spare the rod and make music mild. Some shadow box their many charges, hitting under the belt and landing left hooks with assurance. Most, however, in some way, cue the musicians. Some "Keeping time, time, time, / In a sort of Runic rhyme" erode the music. And then, AND THEN, there are those who conduct the melodic line, ignoring rhythm and counterpoint. Coral was one of these. Her arms flailed in a manner that excited the audience, but left the orchestra members to fend for themselves.

Badger watched and listened. The single double bass violinist standing back toward the alto section of the chorus, playing with a French bow, made him wince. To his professorial mind only the German bow made music come alive on the greatest of all lyric instruments. Few knew the beauty of the rhapsodies of deep bass tones, for few had ears sensitive enough to hear them. Badger listened to the base violin echoing an octive below the sounds of the powerful but few bass voices and was soon lost in the beauty of the music and lost his surroundings.

At the end of the performance the spectators, not sure whether they were a congregation in church or an audience in a theatre, finally gave in and applauded wildly then moved rapidly to the stairs leading to the recreation room below where the ladies' society was serving coffee and tea and some home made cookies. Badger and Mary found Father Jack and had their talk with him before he was whisked off by a group of sodality ladies.

"I think it just as well that we didn't have coffee earlier at your place, Johnny," said Bernadine when Badger returned from the line with a tray of cookies, three coffees and a tea.

"Where is Coral?" asked Mary. "I would like to congratulate her. That was a beautiful performance."

"It was indeed," agreed Blanche. "I would think that she would be down here. All of the singers are." Looking around, they could see all of the black and blue and white, although most of the ties had been removed.

"She certainly isn't down here," said Bernadine. "It would be difficult to miss her in that red dress."

"That's probably it," said Mary. "She is somewhere changing out of the dress. I doubt that she would want to wear it anywhere other than when she is conducting."

"Enjoy the concert?"

They looked around to see Edmund Linehan standing with several ladies, whom he introduced as his wife and one of his daughters. His large frame next to the various sizes of the others made the group appear to any observer, if there were any, like the Sears Tower and surrounding Chicago buildings. Actually no one was observing them. The room was filled with people too busy observing themselves.

"Strange, I don't see Dr. Lehr anywhere," said Edmund. "He is usually the first one in line for coffee and cookies."

"Well, Edmund, I see you are with your usual bevy of beauties!"

Edmund spun around, saw no one so turned back to the group, bewildered.

"Don't keep looking up there, Edmund. Look down here with the common man," came the voice of Onorio Flores.

"Charlie!" said Edmund and Badger in unison. "We didn't see you come in. We didn't even know you were here."

"Of course you didn't," said Onorio, "but I did. I know where I am at all times."

"Where is your wife, Onorio?" asked Bernadine, "We would love to meet her."

"Oh, Margarita? She is over in line getting some more cookies. Speaking of where is, where is Coral? I haven't seen her down here."

"We've decided she is somewhere changing out of her dress into something more subdued," said Blanche.

"Stranger than that," said Edmund, "We haven't seen Karl since the concert, and this is his church."

"I didn't see him *at* the concert," said Blanche. "After he made his speech he went back through the door to the vestry and I didn't see him return."

"Neither did I," said Mary. "Did you, Badger?"

"He didn't come back in by that door. Maybe he went around to the back from outside or through the basement and listened from there," said Badger. "That would be better than walking in front of the chorus. Ah, here may be the answer or at least part of it."

George and the other two ushers entered the crowded room. The two went immediately to the refreshment table. George, on the other hand, looked around, spotted the group, and then walked over to them.

"I really didn't know that ushering meant picking up all of the programs and straightening up the church. Anyone seen Coral?"

"We thought she might be changing her dress," said Mary.

"Not on your life! That's her favorite dress.

Besides, she could have changed a dozen dresses since the concert. Hasn't anyone seen her?"

"Afraid not, George," said Badger. "Also, we haven't seen Dr. Lehr."

"Oh, I just saw him. When I went out to throw the trash in the bin he was carrying a box out from the vestry to his new car. He said something about returning something. He told me he'd be back in a little while, at any rate before we all left. He has to close up the church, you know."

Standing in one place was becoming a problem for Bernadine because of her arthritic pain. So they found a long table which was practically empty, and sat down. Onorio's wife joined them, while George went off looking for Coral.

"There just seems to be one mystery pilled upon another, this Easter week-end," said Bernadine. "I wonder how many of them we won't solve.

CHAPTER XVIII

EASTER NIGHT

What a wild room
We enter, when the gloom
Of windowless night
Shuts us from the light
　　　"A Man-Made World,"　　Stephen Spender

𝔗ime passes rapidly or slowly not according to earth's rotation or any of the mythology we learn in school, but according to a rigid set of scientific rules that treat the pleasure - relaxation / malaise - anxiety relationships to the chemical reaction and the mechanism of Big Ben's older sister in Greenwich. The time passed very slowly indeed for the Badger sisters, Mary and also Badger, whereas Edmund and Onorio, seeing nothing particularly sinister in Coral's disappearance, had the minute hands on their watches spinning like the wheels of a Mario Andretti racer. George, whose minute and second hands were paralyzed, moved from one group to another looking and asking, all to no avail.

Mary whispered to Badger, "Do you think it possible that Coral is with Dr. Lehr?"

"Having the two of them missing does seem strange, but I don't see how there could be a relationship. Coral's disappearance is more coincidence than anything, I'm sure, but I do think we had better start searching for her, if I only knew where."

Badger looked around the room and saw that a great many of the tables were empty and few people were standing. The ladies at the refreshment table were starting to pack up the remaining cookies of which there were now very few. Badger looked at his watch and decided that it was time to take Bernadine and Blanche back up to Lueker hall. When he suggested that they retire for the evening he was greeted by an uproar that made the unpleasantness experienced by Capt. Bligh into a boat ride in the park. The idea was promptly dropped and in its place came the suggestion that they gather all of the Archives committee members and Graham's friends to their table for a rehashing, since Bernadine and Blanche were sure that the departure of Coral was somehow related to the book thefts and murders. There was some difficulty in getting Gary Jurgenson to stay but he finally did. The wives and daughters and friends took another table so everyone was set to start, or almost.

"Where is Graham?" asked Onorio.

"I don't believe this concert was compulsory," said James Craig. "He's probably at home biting his fingernails."

"Graham wasn't at the concert," said Edmund. "I don't think he was in a frame of mind for music.

George jumped up. "I'm going over to his place. That's where Coral must be."

Badger grabbed George's coat and held him. "Wait a minute. Let's not go running off. Charlie, could you call Graham and ask him to get down here?"

Margarita stood up from the next table. "I'll go,

Charlie. You stay here and have your meeting." She walked over to the corner of the room where a telephone sat on a desk.

Badger turned and yelled, "Margaret, perhaps you had better call Sgt. Reburg of the state police and ask him to come over here, too."

"Okay, I'll get him. Sgt. who?"

"Sgt. Reburg." He turned back to the table "I think it would make sense if we moved beyond where we were at the last meeting with a quick up date. The Quincy police have found the books that were stolen outright as well as 'The Question.' They were all in Jack Zinecor's home. So the missing books are down to four:*The Scarlet Letter, Wieland, The Spy,* and *The History of the Town of Plymouth.* These are the four that had some form of forgeries substituted in the Archives and are the books that the criminal originally wanted and that he had Sermons steal for him.

"On the surface I would agree," said Dennis Marlin, lighting a cigarette, "but with that view I think we are saying Larry Sermons took all the books, some for the forger and others for himself. "Are we then saying that Sermons was killed by the forger? Why?"

"Because Sermons' thefts uncovered those forgeries," said Edmund. "Although I must admit that Graham's finding the forged *Scarlet Letter* while looking for *The People, Yes* seems very strange."

"His absence tonight doesn't exactly appear decorous," said Blanche.

Gary Jurgenson sat back in his chair and took

a sip of the coffee that was by now quite cold. He smiled a knowing smile. "So we seem to have the following scenario: Zinecor made forgeries then hired Sermons to put them in the Archives and take the originals. Sermons decided to take some books on his own. When Graham discovered the missing books because Sermons had taken *The People, Yes,* Zinecor got mad and killed him and took all the books. "

"Where, then, are those four really valuable books?" Asked James Craig. Mr. Badger didn't say anything about the Quincy police finding them."

"The name is Badger, not Mr. Badger." said Blanche.

"Yes, of course," said Craig, with a wry smile. "Where, Gary, are the four books, if your theory is correct?"

"Zinecor had plenty of time to hide them. I've never been in his home so I don't know exactly where they could have been. They were probably taken by his killer. I certainly would like to know who it was who killed Jack Zinecor, and why? After all, he may have had his flaws but he was a colleague in books and interest in books."

"*Who* is our biggest question," said Edmund. "I suspect the *Why* was to get the books. Whoever it was figured out that Zinecor had them, made arrangements to meet him in that classroom and killed him."

A slight noise by the stairs caused almost everyone to turn around. Dr. Lehr and Sgt. Reburg entered the room together, Reburg with his right hand on his pistol butt and Dr. Lehr with his left hand swinging an ever present cane, this one with a bulldog head.

"Good evening, you two," Greeted Badger. "It sure didn't take you long to get here, Chuck."

"What are you mumbling about, Badger?"

"About getting here in a hurry from the time that Charlie's wife called you."

"I didn't get any call. I came over here because I just saw Jean Jederman at the stop sign and she said you were over here. I thought someone with authority should be present." He and Dr. Lehr took seats.

"Where is Coral Reiser?" asked the doctor. "I thought she'd be back by now."

"Back from where?" asked George.

"Why, when she finished her concert and all her charges were out of the vestry, she poked her head into my office and said she had to run home for a minute and would be right back."

"Do you have any idea why she had to go home, Dr. Lehr?" asked Sgt. Reburg.

"She didn't say, but my guess is that she had to change her dress. I can't be sure, but it looked to me as if she had grease or something on it. Some of those brass players use a greasy lubricant on their instruments, especially that Billye Renwick and everyone was brushing up against her as they were leaving the sanctuary."

"You see, she'll be here any minute," said Blanche, trying to soothe the frazzled nerves of George. "If she got grease on her dress she would want to wash it out right away. That takes time."

"She may have gotten grease on herself and decided to take a bath," said Charlie. "Hey, Margarita, did you think to call Coral?"

"She's not listed in the phone book."

"I'm sure she will be here soon. What is it you all are doing here?" asked Dr. Lehr. "Besides relaxing after the concert, I mean. This looks like a meeting of the Archives committee, sans Coral and Graham."

"Sans Coral only," said a voice at the end of the table. Graham Carruth plopped into a chair. "I got your message, and I repeat Karl's question: What is it you are all doing here? The concert is over and all decent people are off the streets and out of the churches."

"We were trying to bring everyone up to date on our mystery," said Badger, "and Mr. Jurgenson was giving us his theory of the case."

"To put it all in a nut shell," said Jurgenson, "I believe that Zinecore hired Sermons to take the books, but Sermons took extra books and was killed for it. Then Zinecor was killed by someone who stole the books from him, maybe one of his Goodman colleagues."

"I hope that your theory is correct," said Marlin, "because then we could all supply our alibis. Whoever didn't have one would be the guilty party."

A large smile filled Sgt. Reburg's face. "I really don't believe that the case is quite that simple, Mr. Marlin. But let's go on. Anyone have any other ideas?

"I think Zinecor was bamboozled just like Larry Sermons was," said Graham. "I've known him for years and he wouldn't do anything dishonest. I wouldn't have asked him to help in this matter if I had the least notion that he would steal anything. I think Badger's theory about Jack stealing Twain's 'The Question' is poppycock."

"Do you mean to sit there and say that Larry Sermons was victimized by someone?" said Charlie. "If you do, then you're the only person in all of Walden who doesn't know he was a cheap, two bit thief."

"What I meant was . . . . ." But that was as far as Graham was able to get. Almost everyone was speaking at once on the topic of Larry Sermons' virtue, proving in this sampling far better than Gallup ever could that Sermons was a horse thief, highwayman, crook, and swindler.

"Badger, we've heard from almost everyone else tonight. Why don't you tell us your theory?" asked Chuck Reburg.

"Yes, Johnny told us earlier today that he knew who it was who murdered Mr. Sermons and Zinecor," said Blanche. "Isn't that right, Johnny?"

Badger had trouble thinking of anything but Graham's diction. "Poppycock! right. At the time I didn't think I could prove it, but now I think I can." The table became quiet. Had the proverbial pin been dropped it would have sounded like an Elvis fan club meeting.

"We have gone over the facts in the case so many times they're ingrained in all of our minds. It seems clear that the criminal isn't a complete stranger and so is someone familiar with the college, the Archives, and the various people on and off campus who've been involved, in a word, US, or one of the faculty who is in town but keeping a distance from this group."

"So far you haven't said anything that hasn't been said over and over by everyone else," said James Craig.

"True, but now maybe I will. We have all been assuming that the criminal forged the books and had Sermons do the dirty work so that he could have the books for himself, except, of course, Mr. Marlin, who said the other day that he knew of stores where he was sure the books could be sold."

"Now wait a minute," Marlin said in a low, teeth gritting voice, "I said that I had been in places where I believed shady dealings went on. That doesn't mean that I would deal with such people."

"No one is accusing you of anything," said Badger. "If anything, I was paying you a complement, because I believe that the murderer of Larry Sermons and Jack Zinecor did not intend to keep the books for himself but to sell them. This was someone who needed money."

"That fits most of us here," said Edmund. "The salaries at Carlton-Stokes or any small college for that matter are not ones that would make anyone rich."

"You misunderstand me, Edmund. I said *needed* money not wanted money. Even some very wealthy people need money when all they possess is tied up and some emergency arises. People may steal when they want something, but I think that murder goes more closely with need."

The wives, children, and friends at the other table were now all silent and all of the other tables were empty. None of the Archives committee members were cognizant of the quiet which pervaded the room except for Bernadine, Blanche, and Mary, who were not on the committee and were certain they should not be interrupting. The high windows on the sides of the room with their deep wells were now black, for none of the outside lights of the church remained on and no passing automobiles shone light down to this basement. It was as if the room were windowless, but all these atmospheric changes were not noticed by the members, who continued to theorize. Voices rose so that no one paid attention to anyone else.

George couldn't keep his mind on Badger's ideas. He was thinking of Coral and beginning to lose faith in Dr. Lehr's theory that she was at home changing her dress. He unobtrusively left the table and walked over to the phone. Coral's number may not have been in the phone book, but it was certainly in George's head. He dialed the number and waited, and waited. After ten rings he hung up.

"I'm going over to Coral's place and find out what's the matter. There's no answer," he called out, as he ran up the stairs.

*   *   *

If there is anything in our world that all men fear, the brave, the cowardly, the callus, it is that the unknown has stricken someone we love. George Mercater was as brave as most men, which means he was braver than a good many. When he left the basement of the Church of Redemption he was shaking with apprehension. When he returned some twenty minutes later he was quaking with total panic. He almost tripped as he came down the stairs. The noise roused the wives, children, and friends at the one table and interrupted the men at the table, who had advanced their theory not one baby step from where it had been when George left. Their melee would have put European soccer fans to shame.

"Coral isn't at her place and hasn't been there since before the concert." George almost yelled as he reached the table. "And her landlady is positive. We've got to do something!"

Reburg jumped up. "Who saw her last?"

He was greeted by mass confused. "We all were," George said, "at the concert. She was directing and we were all there in the audience watching her. Then she . . .No, wait a minute. Dr. Lehr saw her after that in his office."

"We know that, George," said Badger. "What Chuck wants to know is, did anyone see her after that, say Mr. Marlin going out after the concert for a smoke, or Graham doing whatever you were doing this evening?" Badger didn't want to point out the absence of Graham, he just wanted someone to pick up on what he was really saying or trying to say. No one did.

"If Dr. Lehr was the last person to see her and she was going home, then she disappeared between here and her place. Perhaps you had better come with me, George, to show me where she lives. By the way, what kind of car was she driving?"

"She wasn't driving a car. Her landlady drove her and I was going to drive her home afterwards. If she got grease on her dress then she would have walked home. It's only a few blocks."

"Or somebody gave her a lift," said the sergeant. "Come on, we better get going."

"I think that under the circumstance we should adjourn and I will close up the church," said Karl Lehr. "Perhaps we could all meet tomorrow morning in the Archives."

"Not me," said Gary Jurgenson, glancing over at his wife at the other table, who was shaking her head. "Lorraine and I have a long drive home and it's late. I've no intention of driving down here again for awhile. Easter Monday may be a day off for all of you people in your ivory towers, but it's a work day for us."

"Most of the others agreed to meet in the Archives at ten o'clock and started to leave. Badger helped Bernadine out of her chair and walked between her and Blanche, helping both of them. Mary held onto Bernadine's other arm."

"Oh, Mr. Smith, Badger, if I may," said Dr. Lehr. "I would like to congratulate you on your engagement to such a lovely young lady."

The four turned around and thanked the doctor. "I'm sure we are going to be very happy," said Mary. "Walden is such a lovely and friendly town. "Everyone has been so nice to all of us that . . . . ."

"Oh, how stupid of me!" broke in Dr. Lehr. "Here I try to get everyone in the Archives tomorrow, completely forgetting that I have some very important business to take care of in the morning. I don't know when I'll get free. Well, just start without me and I'll try to get there just as soon as I possibly can. I'm sure that you can get along without me. Maybe do even better."

Bernadine and Blanche with Mary and Badger following them were the last to leave the church, except for Dr. Lehr, who was in the basement turning out lights. Once they were in Badger's car and the motor and heater were on to take the chill out of the late evening air, Bernadine turned to Badger with a look that she saved for special occasions.

"Is it too late for a night cap," she said.

Badger looked at his watch. "Quarter of twelve. Just about a perfect time for a brandy. But I would like to make a quick little drive around to see if there is anything going on or if Chuck and George have found Coral."

The four drove all over Walden and found it to be very quiet. Few houses had any lights burning and almost no cars were on the street except those parked for the night at the curb. Sgt. Reburg's police car was nowhere in sight, which seemed not at all unusual and the Church of Redemption was now dark and quiet. Dr. Lehr had undoubtedly finished his light extinguishing task. The quiet night meant there was no reason at all to delay the night cap, so the three women preceeded Badger into his apartment once more, seated themselves comfortably and waited to be served.

"I think, Badger, that you have a great deal of

explaining to do to your fiancee and your sweet old maid aunts," said Bernadine.

"Yes, I guess I have," admitted Badger. "I was sure that my stalling would fool all of the other people tonight, but I knew it would not fool you. When Blanche said that I had told you that I knew who the murderer was I had to stall for time. I am sure I know who did it but proving it is another matter, so I had to let everyone get just a little upset, but then George's patience ran out. When he left to find Coral everyone forgot about my theory, everyone except you. So then we had a mild form of pandemonium."

"Wouldn't it have been better if you had exposed the killer and forced his hand?" said Mary. "That always seems to work in all the movies I've seen."

"That was my plan, but the disappearance of Coral changed all that. I believe she is in real danger right now. That's why I kept quiet ."

"But why would anyone want to harm someone like Coral? How could she be a threat to anyone?"

"Because she knows something, or, much more likely, she saw something. Look at what we all saw and know. Coral conducted*The Creation*, Then, after her bows, exited through the vestry door. She then held it open as first the chorus and then the orchestra exited. After this we know nothing. I'm sure Chuck will start questioning members of the chorus and orchestra, but I doubt that will help. The likely scenerio is that the chorus members went straight through the other door to the outside and came around to the front door of the church and down to the basement room or maybe went straight home.

The orchestra members would take a few moments longer to put their instruments in their cases but would also leave quickly, as there were not really enough of them to call themselves an orchestra, not even a studio orchestra."

"What about Coral putting her head in to tell Dr. Lehr that she was going home? Do you think she did that?" asked Blanche.

"I am sure that that is true. I've never seen his office but I'm sure that some light would show under the door so she would see that he has there. Knowing her, there seems little chance that she wouldn't go in and thank the doctor for the use of his church."

"So we are right back where we started, aren't we, Johnny?" said Bernadine. "Although I must admit that I have a good many more questions on human behavior than I did earlier."

"If they are the same questions that I have," said Blanche, "I would surely like them answered."

"I don't understand how the pastor of a church could host a musical event such as we heard tonight, introduce the performance, then go back to his office to do who knows what?"

"If you remember," said Mary. "He told us as we were leaving that he had important business to complete in the morning. I would imagine that the two are related."

"Of course, you are undoubtedly correct," said

Bernadine.

"Then you believe that his strange disappearance after the concert, with no explanation, is also related to his important morning business?" asked Blanche.

"It does seem the most reasonable explanation," said Mary. "I can't bring myself to think ill of this distinguished elderly gentleman."

"Nor can I," said Bernadine.

"Nor I," agreed Blanche.

"How is this helping us to find Coral?" asked Mary.

"It may be helping a great deal," said Bernadine. "Every little detail or question that we bring out in the open helps, doesn't it, Johnny?"

All three ladies looked at Badger, who was staring off in space.

Bernadine smiled and sipped from her snifter. "Yes, I think that we may have helped a great deal. I suppose we should all be getting back to our rooms. Who would like to wake Johnny?"

*   *   *

The ride back to Lueker Hall was not uneventful. The driver had certainly not had anywhere near the amount of alcohol in his system that the young princess' chauffeur had had, but he was totally intoxicated with ideas, ideas which often disturb a driver's ability to see, hear, and think in terms of the mundane thoughts of Twentieth Century automobiles. No tunnel walls were scraped - nor did any photograhers snap scandalous pictures of the lovely Lady Mary, but Badger did manage to strike a number of curbs and jolt both his aunts and his lovely fiancee. They were, nevertheless, home in a very short time, a time that helped Badger to understand where, what, and who he was.

After his aunts were reluctantly put to bed, Badger walked Mary out on the campus, showing her not the beauty of the noon or the stars, but the beauty of the moon and stars as they shone above Carlton - Stokes College and the town of Walden just below it.

"Sometimes, Johnny, I can't tell whether it is me you love or a logic problem or murder mystery."

"If you have any doubts at all, I think I can clear them up on our honeymoon and for a lifetime afterward."

"That almost sounds like something out of Twentieth Century Fox."

"I think they stole it from me. It doesn't matter. Whatever, I love you, and always will."

Only the most cynical would doubt the two. They walked over the campus until the dew told them it was time for Mary to go to sleep and Badger to go to work. A good night kiss was all that this night required. And Badger staggered over to his car, feeling the joy that he thought was only reserved for a teen-ager. He started the engine and backed out, bumping a dumpster directly behind him, pulled forward and managed to get his car down the road to town. No man should ever have to deal with the kind of love he fealt for Mary and the excitement of a murder mystery all in the same night, especially when he was required to maneuver an automobile.

As Badger drove down the Hill he knew the night was even more quiet than it had been earlier. He also knew what he had to do, and his stomach tightened at the thought. He drove down to the highway and turned left. At one o'clock in the morning he did not expect to see anyone on the highway, but he was mistaken. On the corner, by the bank there stood Doug Boito, looking like Shorty in *The Most Happy Fella*, but there were no girls going by.

"Doug, what in the world are you doing here at after one in the morning?" he called out.

Doug walked up to the window and leaned in. "Oh, you, Prof. Smith! Waitin' for Lauderdale. Fixed his Bank's drain pipe an' he ran off for somethin'. Give me a ride home, okay?" He didn't wait for an answer but opened the door and got in.

"If you were willing to help that Merrill Lauderdale, how about delaying sleep just a little more and helping me?"

"What you got in mind? Want to rob his bank?"

Badger smiled. "You're not too far from it. I want to break into a church." He waited a moment to let his statement sink in.

"A church, huh? Well then I believe I'd better

start calling you Badger. Want to tell me a few of the details. It'll be easier for me when I try explainin' it to the judge."

"The Church of Redemption. I was going to break in alone, but I'm sure I'd make quite a racket. With you fate handed me a real helpmate. You could get in without the noise. I need to check a few things, Okay?"

Badger drove down several blocks then turned left again. He turned off his headlights a few hundred yards before they reached the church and put the gearshift in neutral then turned off the motor. The slight incline allowed them to glide to the vestry door with no difficulty.

The two got out of the car both on the passenger side. While Doug went to the vestry door Badger took his flashlight from the glove compartment, put a piece of paper in the jamb and closed the door silently. Doug took out his pen light and examined the lock. He tried several keys without success, put them away then used his jack knife. The lock clicked, Doug stepped aside, and Badger pulled open the door and the two men entered the church, where neither one had any intention of praying.

CHAPTER XIX

MONDAY MORNING

No law
But the law of deprivation.

No hope
But the hope of deliverance.
"The Face I Know,"   Brother Antoninus

There is a law of nature and of philosophy, and of the spirit, a law so common that no one bothers to write it down. Without this law our civilization would crumble further into the dust than it already has. Because most of the characters and places in this narrative may appear real (although most of them are fictional) this law once more must remain unexpressed. But, dear reader, you know what it is, as did Badger.

When Doug and Badger entered the vestry they were both apprehensive, Badger because he had a good idea what to expect and Doug because he had no idea. Badger closed the door and then turned off his flashlight and looked around. Complete darkness. No light shone anywhere. The sound was as black as the sight. There were no windows. He turned the flashlight back on and washed it over the walls. Nothing unusual. The room was triangular with one wall fitting against the sanctuary with its door. Several large closets were against one wall. Each one was examined and found to hold a variety of church vestments. A table surrounded by a number of chairs occupied most of the floor space. In one of the corners stood an ornate door. It was locked. Badger stepped aside and Doug stepped forward, where he applied his jack knife, and then stepped back. Badger pushed the door open. It gave off the signature sound of "The Inner Sanctum," for those who are old enough to remember, and Doug surely was.

"Nothing of interest here," said Doug, as if he knew why they were there or what they were looking for.

The flashlight once again was washed over the room where a large desk in the middle dominated. One high backed chair was behind it while two smaller ones faced it. Badger's visage altered when he saw that the desktop was almost bare. Only a blotter, pen set, and lamp were visible. This was not what he expected. The drawers held nothing unusual. This room, too, was triangular, for it occupied the opposite side of the sanctuary. A long narrow stained glass window, Badger remembered seeing from the outside, gave character to one of the three walls while large bookcases filled with primarily rich volumes of religious tracts covered the other two walls, except where a door intervened. Given the design of the building, this had to be a closet. Badger turned the handle. This door also was locked. The jack knife did its job. This time Doug opened the door and let Badger step forward and shine the light inside. Both men looked in at the same time.

"Oh my God! It's Coral!"

"Miss. Reiser! What's goin' on here?"

Badger dropped to his knees before the body of Coral Reiser lying on the floor of the closet in a fetal position. Her red dress was torn about the neck and sleeves. The decorative sash was tied tightly over her bruised mouth, giving her a grotesque smile. Thick black cords bound her hands and feet. She was clearly not conscious, perhaps dead. Badger fealt for a pulse. There was one.

"Who would do that to a lovely lady like Miss Reiser?" said Doug. "And after that holy concert she gave. We better pull her out here so we can see to untie her."

The body was pulled out of the closet. There being no need for secrecy any longer, Badger turned the desk lamp switch but nothing happened. Doug flicked the wall switch and the overhead ceiling light flooded the room. The ruptured lamp cord told them where some of the bonds came from to tie up Coral. The two removed the sash and cord, but Coral remained comatose. Black and blue marks on either side of her mouth and on her wrists and ankles attested to her recent captivity. She had a large bump on the side of her head.

"You wonder why the guy didn't just strangle her," said Doug.

"Smashing Larry Sermons or shooting Jack Zinecor are one thing, but a gentleman doesn't kill a lady, if he can help it."

"Better phone Doc Peacock," said Doug as he picked up the phone book from the stand next to the desk. He found the number, picked up the phone and put it to his ear for several seconds. "Dead."

"Now we know where the rest of the cord

came from," said Badger, fingering the short wire sticking from the phone like a doctor looking at the umbilical cord of a new born child. "Ripped out of the wall and cut out of here." There's a pay phone in the vestibule. I'll go call."

"Doc don't like to be called up in the middle of the night. It's better comin' from an old friend. I'll go call him."

Before Badger could move, Doug had grabbed the flashlight and was on his way out the door. "You stay here with Miss Reiser. I'll be right back."

Badger tried rubbing Coral's hands but it didn't seem to help. He knew better than to try forcing brandy down her throat, besides there was no brandy anywhere in sight. There wasn't even any wine that he could see. He went back into the vestry and opened the closet, took out a number of heavy robes and carried them back to cover Coral, then he wadded up others and put them under her head. He remembered about shock. All he could do now was wait.

Looking about the room he saw that the walls held the greatest interest so examined the bookcases and all the books in them. He even took some books out of each shelf and felt behind to see if anything was there. There was something there, dust, and something else. He pulled it out, looked at it, smiled, then wrapped the heavy shiny object in his handkerchief and put it in his pocket. No need to look any further.

"Doc'll be here in a few minutes. Didn't seem too pleased to be gettin' calls this time in the mornin'." Doug Boito was standing in the doorway. "You know my Agnes? She's about as curious as any cat I ever saw.   Just in case my Agnes   should bring up the subject, care to tell me what's goin' on here."

"I thought that I'd find those missing books from the Archives here, Doug. The reasons for that are kind of mixed up right now.   But fool that I am, it never occurred to me that I'd find Coral here.   She must have stumbled   across something,   maybe even the books, and Dr. Lehr did this to her."

"Dr.Lehr?   That nice elderly gentleman.   Why, he's a reverend.   Baptised my brother's boy. He wouldn't do such a thing. You must have the wrong man."

"I'm afraid not. It was Dr. Lehr all right. Hit her on the back of the head when she came into this office after the concert.   Wait a minute! If he tied her up and left her here he must not intend to come back."   Badger started to panic.   "He must be on the highway right now.   He could be out of state."

"If you are right and Dr. Lehr did do this, you don't have to worry about his being out of state. I'd say he's still in Walden.   A little before you came by the bank Dr. Lehr, or at least his car, passed by goin' the other way.   He was in that big, new Buick of his. I saw his tail lights make a sharp right a couple a blocks after the stop light   right   at Prentice St.   That's where Gertrude Grant lives alone with her two cats. Scuttlebutt has it that he's been seein' her quite a few times of an evenin' ever since her second husband expired."

"Her husband what?"

"You know, died. He passed on last summer after his third heart attack.   Far as I can see, the only reason Dr. Lehr would be drivin' down Prentice St. would be to see Gertie. There's nothin' else on that street to interest a man like him. If he was going to get out of town he'd want to talk her into goin' with him. Not an easy job. He'd need lots of time and lots and lots of money for that, if I know Gertie, and I do."

"Doug, could you stay here with Coral and wait for the doctor? I have to get word to the police, and I don't mean Wash Rutan."

"Why not? It'll give me more to tell my Agnes, just in case she brings up the subject some cold winter mornin' over coffee."

Badger ran from the office into the vestry, through the door into the church, up the aisle to the vestibule and the wall phone that hung there. He extracted change from his pocket, this time finding the coins he needed, dropped them into the slot, and dialed O.

"Get me Cellular phone number, ah. . . ah." Badger hesitated then reached into his wallet where he had put the note paper with Reburg's number on it and gave the number to the operator.

A voice answered on the first ring, "Sgt. Reburg."

"Chuck, this is Badger. You've got to meet me on the corner of the highway and Prentice St. as fast as you can. I'll explain then."

"Where in blazes is Prentice St.?" In small towns like Walden very few people besides the mailman and Doug Boito know names of streets.

"Two or three blocks south of the stop light," said

Badger, who knew the street location only because of the way Doug had described Lehr's car turning. "Hurry."

"Where are you?"

"At the Church of Redemption."

"I'll be there before you are."

Badger hung up, retraced his steps and left by the vestry door, yelling a good bye to Doug. He made as much noise pulling his car out as he had created silence pulling it in. The houses and parked cars along the street down to the highway were a blur to Badger. All of the street lights on the highway business district, or Fourth St., passed without any notice at all. Chuck Reburg was waiting in his car at the corner of the highway facing Prentice St. Badger leaned over to the passinger side and both men rolled down their windows.

"Told you that I'd beat you here," said Chuck. "I was the next block over watching for any cars coming down the hill. None came unless I was asleep. Now what's going on? You know anything about Miss Reiser. That George Mercater is going crazy!"

Badger parked his car and climbed in with Reburg, made a quick explanation of what he thought had happened and what he had just experienced. The two drove slowly up Prentice St. looking for a new Buick, a rather easy task in a town where the Ford dealer came in second only to his own used car lot. The black Buick was parked on the left side of the street in front of a house with lights on the front porch.

"That must be it," said Badger, pointing to the car.

Chuck Reburg switched off his lights and eased his police car behind the Buick and turned off the motor. He took his pistol out of the holster.

"If you are right about this guy, and it looks like you are, then I may have to use the threat of this. I want you to go into the back yard. Find a garbage can lid and a stick or anything you that will made noise. Then hide. When I ring the bell he may decide to exit the back way. If he does, stay hidden but make a racket to scare him back into the house. If he comes out, just let him get away. He can't go far."

The two got out of the car and closed the doors very quietly. Badger walked rapidly to the rear of the house while Chuck gave him time. There was no garbage can, but there was a tricycle on the lawn of the next house over. Badger crept over to the house and looked carefully. There it was with a bell on the handlebars. He picked it up and carried it to a spot next to the porch. On the ground lay a large branch, which he also commandeered. Remembering that Jack Zinecor was shot with a twenty-two, he hid himself well under the porch and waited, and waited and waited. Earlier in this narrative something was said about time moving rapidly or slowly according to one's sense of pleasure and pain or degree of apprehension. This certainly applied to Badger under the porch. What little he could see from his vantage point was not enough to suggest the world rotated at all. The ten or fifteen seconds he spent seemed to him like a half hour.

In the distance he heard a bell ring and realized that it was the Grant front door. Time now moved slower than before. There was a complete silence them the back door exploded in sound as it was pulled. Light washed over the porch, through the slats and down to Badger, then drenched the steps and the lawn in cold yellow light.

He beat the stick rapidly against the porch support post and rang the tricycle bell over and over. Unfortunately, Dr. Lehr was one of those rare persons not frightened by the sounds of beating sticks or tricycle bells. He left the house rapidly, confident that his only real danger came from his rear. He came down the steps as fast as he could but not at a run. Ignoring what the sergeant had told him, Badger kicked the tricycle with his foot right into the path of the retreating Dr. Lehr, knocking him to the ground. Lehr tried to reach into his pocket, but Badger was up and ready for him. Using the stick like a gladiator over his vanquished foe he kept the doctor from extracting his gun, for that was indeed what was later found to be in his coat pocket.

"Well, Doctor, I think you had better come along with us. I believe you have quite a bit of explaining to do." Behind Badger was Chuck Reburg holding his own pistol in a manner most nonchalant but nevertheless most threatening.

The two helped Dr. Lehr to his feet and escorted him to the front of the house and the police car where Chuck pulled a piece of paper from the glove compartment and read the doctor his rights. The lights in the bungalow were extinguished, but there was enough illumination from the nearby street light to expose the shadow of Gertrude Grant peaking from behind her curtain at them, just as Dr. Lehr had undoubtedly done just minutes before when the door bell rang.

CHAPTER XX

EASTER MONDAY

The truth is hid and shaped in veils of error
Rich, unanswerable, the profound caught in
plain air.
"Am I My Neighbor's Keeper?"
Richard Eberhart

Badger found it easier to remain up the rest of the night, rather than get comfortable in his bed and fall asleep only to be awakened in an hour or two by the voice in Quincy bringing him the weekly weather revelations followed by basketball, baseball, and hockey scores. Remaining up was also easier because there were many thoughts buzzing around in his head, just like flies caught between window panes, that sleep would have been troubling. So Badger stayed awake at his kitchen table, drinking coffee and once more returning to the cigarettes he had so couragiously abandoned the last several days.

When he and Chuck Reburg took Dr. Lehr down to the Walden jail they decided not to try interrogating him at the time, but to let him become accustomed to the bars that would confine him for the rest of his life, in the hopes that he would be more cooperative in the morning. Two state police officers were called in to guard the prisoner and to make sure that Wash Rutan would not walk into the station in the morning, give the doctor a lecture on drunk driving, and let him go.

Chuck had asked Badger to bring Mary and the Badger sisters to the jail at ten sharp and said he would inform all of the other Archives members and involved parties, which meant Jurgenson, Marlin, and Craig. He was sure that it would be easier to get a confession from Dr. Lehr if everyone was involved. A phone call to Dr. Peacock was met with a terse answer from his wife. This led Badger to drive by the Church of Redemption where he found Dr. Peacock and Doug Boito leading a weak and Confused Coral Reiser out the vestry door.

"She don't remember a thing," said Doug as his greeting.

"A form of temporary amnesia," explained the doctor. "She is pretty shaken up. Should be better by tomorrow. I'm taking her home with me so my wife can look after her. You tell George not to come sniffing around before tomorrow afternoon, late."

The three helped Coral into the doctor's car then Doug joined Badger and was taken to his home where there seems little doubt that he spent much of the remainder of the night trying to explain to Agnes why he helped Prof. Smith break into a church in the middle of the night.

And now it was morning and Badger, shaved and showered and dressed in a pair of blue slacks and gray shirt was driving up the Hill to meet Mary and his aunts to have breakfast at the Lion's Den. He looked forward to telling about his experiences the night before.

"Johnny!" came three voices as he stepped into the Lion's Den and every head in the room turned and Badger walked with his head down.

Mary got up from the booth and met him half way, threw her arms around his neck and kissed him. "Johnny, what you and Mr. Boito did last night was wonderful. We are all so proud of you!" She kissed him again then took his hand and led him back to the booth where he was greeted and kissed by his aunts. In due time Badger learned that Doug Boito had been on campus already that morning and had woven a story that may have lacked complete veracity in places related to Doug's activities but made up for it with its aura of verisimilitude, suspence, and heroism. When the ladies learned that they were to be a part of the interrogation team they were even more impressed and happy.

Breakfast this morning was not served by the smiling Jessica but by the beaming Sania, who as an English and communications major was happy to wait on any member of the English department. She found no difficulty in serving eggs over easy with bacon and orange juice to Bernadine, eggs over hard with sausage links and grape juice to Blanche, French toast with sausage patties and tomato juice to Mary, and a cheese omelette with grapefruit juice to Badger, and coffee for all. The difficulty arose when she brought the check and didn't know who to give it to. Badger finally won out and the group headed down to the Walden police station and its two cells, one with Dr. Lehr as guest.

The Walden police and fire station was just one block away from Badger's apartment and on the same side of the street. There was just enough room on the side of the one story building to park two cars, and two cars were already parked there, so Badger used this as an excuse and let the ladies out. He drove around the corner and down the street to the bank. He checked his watch, still plenty of time. He entered the bank and smiled. The cashier at the first station was a former student, a Miss Turek. After talking to her he went to the back to have a few words with Charlie's wife.

A short time later he parked his car and walked to the police and fire station. The front of the building held a single fire engine and a number of closets to hold the volunteers' fire geer. Behind it with an entrance on the side was the police station which consisted of two desks, four filing cabinets, a long conference table, a bathroom, and two rather antiquated cells, the first of which housed Dr. Karl Lehr. He was sitting on a straight chair facing the outer room where all the members of the Archives committee, save Coral Reiser, were sitting or standing facing him. James Craig and Dennis Marlin had taken chairs directly in front of the cell, so were only a few feet from Dr. Lehr's sullen face. Gary Jurgenson was leaning against an old fashioned iron radiator, while one of the two state policemen along with Wash Rutan were all the way back against the fire house wall. The other policeman was by the outer door and opened it as Badger stepped in. A lone man sat by the cell half facing Karl Lehr and half facing the crowd. He wore a suit and had a briefcase in his lap. Chuck Reburg had been thorough. Dr. Lehr was represented by council.

Badger entered and walked over to Chuck Reburg, who stood behind James Craig. Dr. Lehr became quite alert, watching Badger's lips. The room became very quiet even though no one had been talking before.

"I think that we are about ready to start," said Chuck. "I would caution all of you to speak only if called upon. This is not a trial or even a preliminary hearing."

"I object!" said the lawyer. "On what grounds are you holding this hearing?"

"I repeat, Mr. Savitt, this is not a hearing. The police are allowed to interrogate any prisoner. Because so often this happens behind closed doors there are miscarrages of justice and, as a result, innocent men are convicted or guilty ones are freed on technicalities. I wish to have this questioning carried out before many witnesses, including yourself." He paused, looked about, then continued.

"First of all, Dr. Lehr, we know and can prove that you hit and tied up Coral Reiser and left her in the closet of your office. By your own admission yesterday you were the last person to see her before her disappearance. Quite frankly, we have not been able to speak to her, as she has been under Dr. Peacock's care. She's suffered shock. We have been assured that she will be able to answer our questions this afternoon so there is no sense in your wasting time on denials." Dr. Lehr's face fell and his shoulders drooped. "I would like Prof. Smith to take over at this time and give the scenario of the crimes. Badger."

Badger took over as if he were in the classroom lecturing on Robinson's Tilbury Town or Masters' Spoon River. "The first incident of importance, Dr. Lehr, is that you started courting Gertrude Grant after her husband died. In this you became similar to the Reverend Davidson in Somerset Maugham's 'Rain.' A man of morals lured into sin by the wiles of a woman. It did not take you long to realize that she could not be wooed without money, a great deal of money, because she was determined to throw off the small town life for a fast life in the city." Badger was guessing on that one. "The purchase of a new Buick was part of your attempt to impress her. Since you paid for the car by check, your checking and savings accounts are almost depleted. Also, you cashed checks for money to pay Larry Sermons."

"How could you know about his accounts?" cried Mr. Savitt. "Bank accounts are private and . . . ."

"I will get to that shortly, Mr. Savitt," said Badger. "Since there was no way to obtain money in a legitimate fashion, it had to be done illegally. Not an easy task in a town like Walden where the pastor of a major church is known to everybody even if he doesn't know them. All of the valuable books in the Archives of Carlton-Stokes College seemed ideal, as they would bring many thousands of dollars easily obtained in St. Louis, Kansas City, Chicago or even New York rare or second hand book stores, stores that Dr. Lehr frequented on numerous vacations over the years."

Badger turned around and faced the committee. "You may all remember that he told us more than once in our meetings about the questionable activities in some of the shops he frequented. I found it strange that he . . . . ."

Badger twirled around and addressed Karl Lehr. "I found it rather strange that you said nothing the other day when Mr. Marlin mentioned knowing of places that would buy questionable books. However, taking books from the Archives presented certain risks, risks you didn't wish to confront. You didn't wish to steal books and have them discovered missing in a day or two and have the records show that you had been in the Archives recently."

Badger was speaking to Karl Lehr but talking to everyone in the room, turning and gesturing, not like the trial lawyer but like the teacher he was. Mr. Savitt, taken in by the tone and mood of the room raised his hand to speak.

"In good time, Mr. Savitt. The task became a plan when you became aquainted with the reputation and the person of Mr. Larry Sermons. He might try to cheat you but he would not turn you in. And the plan became feasible when you thought of your second edition of *The Scarlet Letter*. Your knowledge of books made changing the second edition to look like the first relatively simple, and you hired Sermons to make the switch. The other books you had him switch were seldom used or checked out so you weren't worried that the poor job at forging them would make any difference."

Badger paused and looked into the eyes of Karl Lehr and knew that so far he was absolutely right. He noticed that Mr. Savitt was also looking at the prisoner and saw the same thing in his eyes. Wash Rutan, coughed in the back of the room, and Badger snapped out of his contemplation.

"Without your knowing it, Larry Sermons stole the other books, intending to peddle them on his own. He had seen Jack Zinecor a number of times on campus and approached him and sold the books, probably at a good price for Zinecor. Because of this and a strange set of circumstances, *The People, Yes* was discovered missing and then*The Scarlet Letter* forgery was found. You were naturally furious. You confronted Sermons Thursday night in the Archives. His attitude infuriated you further and when he turned his back you hit him with your walking stick, the one with the silver head, given to you by your devoted congregation. You had killed Larry Sermons!"

"Now wait just one minute!" Mr. Savitt almost screamed. "This is preposterous. How can you say such a thing?"

"With no difficulty at all." Badger turned around to face the crowd. "I'm sure there isn't a person in Walden who hasn't seen Dr. Lehr walking about town or on campus carrying his silver headed walking stick. His carrying a cane was an affectation everyone in town respected. The head of the stick was certainly heavy enough to strike a man dead. Have you all noticed that that walking stick has been missing from the good doctor's person since Larry Sermons' murder, as has the murder weapon? While Doug Boito and I were going through the doctor's office I also found this!"

He reached into his pocket and pulled out a shiny ball covered by his handkerchief and held it over his head for everyone to see.

"This is the head of the walking stick! It was behind books in his bookshelf. You can see where this bit of splintered wood broke off from the rest of the stick, which is still hidden behind the books."

Karl Lehr hung his head in total defeat and Mr. Savitt simply looked away from everyone in the room. He had to realize that on the technicality of Badger and Doug breaking into the church without a warrant he might be able to have the cane thrown out as evidence when the case came to trial, but in small towns, juries tended to rely more on right and wrong than they often did in the cities.

"After the body of Larry Sermons was discovered by Mary and Doug and me, Zinecor put together a number of things. He figured logically that the one who hired Sermons had to be someone very familiar with the Archives and was probably one of the people at the meetings. Then the theft of Mark Twain's 'The Question' was a very obvious means of bringing the murderer to the fore, because anyone so interested in the stolen books that he would commit murder would want the Twain manuscript and know Zinecor had it."

Three hands shot up, just as in a classroom setting. Badger examined the palms and then the faces of Edmund, Graham, and Gary Jurgenson and called on Edmund as being the one to make his question closest to that which he wanted to answer.

"Somewhere, Badger, you have lost me, and apparently some others as well, if the show of hands means anything. How would Zinecor figure that his theft would be recognized as his doing?"

Badger cleared his throat and prepared for another lecture. "You must remember that Graham said that his helpers and Dr. Lehr were with him at the time the manuscript was placed back in the drawer. They all saw Zinecor handling it. He was the last to touch it so would be the most logical one to have stolen it, either by slight of hand at the time or placing it so that he could get it out of the drawer. This would occur to the perpetrator of the book thefts long before it would occur to anyone else because the guilty are always more likely to suspect someone than are the innocent. At any rate, Zinecor's little subterfuge worked, unfortunately for him."

"But why would anyone want to confront Larry Sermons' killer? Wouldn't that be extremely dangerous?" asked Mary, who had just committed the *faux pas* of not raising her hand.

"I don't believe he realized how dangerous a move it was. I'm sure he thought that the killer would be too frightened of being caught to do anything further. Besides Dr. Lehr is now an elderly man. Exactly what he intended to do we may never know." He turn to the cell. "Unless you would like to tell us. I suspect he was thinking of some form of blackmail. Am I correct, Doctor?"

Dr. Lehr squirmed but said nothing. Mr. Savitt had given up.

"All we need at this point are the missing books and the twenty-two caliber pistol. I'm sure the state police will find them in Dr. Lehr's home, or possibly in Mrs. Gertrude Grant's home, both of which are being searched at this time, under warrant."

Dr. Karl Lehr stood up. "All right, all right, Sergeant. Empty the room and I'll talk. And especially get rid of him." He was pointing to Badger. "Let's have an end to this charade."

Too late the ladies lead Badger from the jail; who had started singing to himself, "You'll be the finest fella in the Easter Charade.

CHAPTER XXI

THE CRUELEST MONTH

O O O O that Shakespeherian Rag —
It's so elegant
So intelligent

"The Waste Land," T. S. Eliot

𝕿he students had started coming back to campus on Sunday night but had not been noticed by Badger or anyone else for that matter, hardly even by themselves. By Monday afternoon, however, it was impossible not to notice them. They swarmed over the campus and the town like Daphne du Maurier's birds on London. They were everywhere, for the most part happy to be back because Carlton-Stokes College was now more their home than the many suburbs of Chicago or St. Louis or any of the towns in between.

The day was spent by Mary, Bernadine, Blanche and Badger in making phone calls, short car trips to the police station, and drinking gallons of coffee served by both Jessica and Sania, all in an attempt to answer some remaining questions. Midway through the sunny afternoon George came into the Lion's Den supporting a still shaky Coral. The group moved to a large table in the center of the room where they had more space but considerably less privacy as all of the students in the Lion's Den were watching them.

Coral sipped tea and munched on a cookie and hesitantly told of her adventures on Easter night.

"When the concert was over I held the door into the vestry for all of the singers and musicians to exit. When they had all left, I switched off the lights and prepared to leave myself, but I noticed light coming from under Dr. Lehr's office door. So I naturally opened that door to tell the doctor good night and to thank him for all of his cooperation. When I stuck my head in I saw him at his desk with some books that he was wrapping carefully in tissue paper and placing in a small box. He was so engrossed in what he was doing that he didn't even notice me until I was right up in front of his desk where I saw him holding the copy of *The Scarlet Letter*."

"You mean it was right there in his hands?" asked Blanche.

"Right in plain sight with those other three books," said Coral, continuing, "When he saw me he gave out a little yelp, almost like a dog, then jumped up and was around the desk before I even had a chance to do anything. He grabbed his desk lamp. I thought he was going to strike me with it, but then he whirled me around and started to strangle me, and I fainted."

"You poor thing," said Mary. "You were very lucky, however. Fainting may have saved your life."

"I think you're right, Mary," said Bernadine. "He must have realized at that point that he could not continue to live in Walden so murdering you had no purpose. I think, also that he was sorry for what he had been doing. After all, he was, or had been, a man of God."

"Exactly, Bernadine," said Badger, "and there was a great deal of difference between killing a ne'er do well like Larry Sermons or a blackmailer like Jack Zinecor and a lady like Coral. I'd say that just about wraps up everything."

"Wait a minute!" four voices almost shouted in unison. Coral was not yet strong enough to shout. "Where are the books?"

"After all, Johnny," said Bernadine. "It was the missing books replaced with forgeries that started this whole affair."

"The state police are still searching Dr. Lehr's home as well as Gertrude Grant's bungalow. It's very much like *Getting Gertie's Garter*, that old bedroom farce. I expect a call from Chuck Reburg at almost any time. He knows where we are. Personally, I favor Grant's place. After Dr. Lehr tied up Coral he took the books to her home, which would explain the delay from the time George saw him and the time he arrived in the basement of his church. If he had taken them to his own home he wouldn't have taken so long. When the books are found, this will certainly establish that Gertie was an accomplice after the fact and, I suspect, *before* the fact as well, not to murder but thefts."

There seemed little to discuss of the crime except a few rather unimportant questions, such as why was it that Badger's, or as his aunts' put it, Johnny's, book was so close to Larry Sermons' body in the Archives? That, as Badger rationalized, was an easy one to answer. Larry Sermons was drawn to anything he recognized, even books, which he recognized something in, and he recognized the name of John Badger Smith. He had no idea what the book was, or what it was worth, so he was probably looking it over when Dr. Lehr interupted his intellectual musings. An argument ensued and Larry Sermons was killed with the silver headed cane, which the doctor, not unexpectedly took with him, thus no murder weapon at the scene."

"You were right, Badger," came the voice of Chuck Reburg from the doorway. "We found the four books at Gertrude Grant's home, just as you thought. There's no question that she was in on this whole thing from the beginning, and in time we'll prove it. Quite the dolls we have in Walden! Did some checking on Mrs. Schmidt. Seems she took a box of personal stuff from under Sermons' bed. She wanted something to remember him by. We won't charge her."

Chuck Reburg scraped a chair from another table and placed it between Badger and Mary. The presence of a uniformed policeman on campus, much less sitting in the Lion's Den was enough to close the mouths of the most vociferous of students, and many were in the room at the time. "Can you guess where the books were?" The sergeant looked around and waited.

"Mixed in with her other books in her bookcase," hazarded Blanche.

"If she had any books, that would have been a good guess. Gertrude Grant is not the intellectual type. You were right, again, Badger, when you made the reference this morning to that missionary in 'Rain' and that girl. What was her name?"

"Sadie Thompson," said Blanche.

Chuck smiled. "Dr. Lehr may be an intellectual, but it wasn't Gertie's mind that attracted him to her. Guess again."

"My guess is that you found the box in the garbage, and if we continue with our literary allusions, the books were in Gertie's lingerie and garter drawer, that is if we can call any play by Al Woods literary," said Badger.

"That is a pretty good job of guessing," said Reburg. "That's exactly where we found them, under her unmentionables. I wonder if she put them there because she thought it a safe place or if Dr. Lehr told her to put them there. You know, the literary allusion stuff."

"I doubt very much," said Blanche, "that Dr. Lehr was in much of a whimsical mood at that time."

"True enough," said Reburg. "We took the doctor over to the county seat. Gertie is now in the doctor's cell down town. I think looking at those bars for a few hours will loosen her tongue."

Chuck Reburg scooted back his chair. "Well that about wraps up this case, I'm very happy to say. I'm due to retire at the end of the month. The college has offered me a job as the security officer so I may be seeing a lot of Badger and Mary, Miss Reiser and Mr. Mercater, that is unless I become city manager of La Grange. It's been nice meeting you, Bernadine and Blanche. I'll see you again at the wedding, that is, if I'm invited. Thank you all for all of your help." He stood, squeezed both Mary's and Badger's shoulders and started for the door, then turned around.

"I did forget something. One of my men did a little checking at the bank, as you suggested, Badger. So now we have another charge for the doctor. He'll be behind bars for the rest of his life." He was out the door and gone.

"Johnny! What is this?" said Bernadine.

"When I saw Doug Boito last night he was by the Walden State Bank. You remember, I told you that Margarita Flores is an officer there, loan department. He said he was there to fix a drain pipe that had burst. The bank president phoned him and asked him to fix it as a favor to him. Outside of automobiles Doug takes care of most of the mechanical problems in this town. Anyway, I told you before that I don't believe in Thomas Hardy's 'Hap' so I did a little investigating. The water pipe didn't just break all by itself. Someone tripped over it in the basement, trying to find the stairs, I think. If you can imagine, that bank has an old fashioned cellar door with no lock. There are, however, no steps. The basement has the furnace and otherwise is used solely as a storage place for Mr. Lauderdale's other businesses, including that electrical shop on Fourth St. It seems that Lauderdale spent his evening taking down Easter decorations, so he brought them to the bank basement, saw the broken pipe and called Doug. When I let you off at the jail this morning I went to the bank. I used my influence with a former student and Charlie's wife to find that Dr. Lehr had been spending a great deal of time around the bank lately. When I saw the basement I informed Chuck of my suspicions and he sent a man over there with finger print equipment. That's it. As Chuck said, We got him. Can you imagine a man like that thinking of burglerizing a bank?"

"Badger, you are always making literary allusions to everything in your life. What book or play were you thinking of that made you suspect Dr. Lehr?" asked Mary.

"I think I can answer that one for you," said Bernadine. "May I, Johnny?" Badger nodded. "It was *The Scarlet Letter.*"

"*The Scarlet Letter* !" said George. "How does that relate other than being one of the stolen books?"

Bernadine continued. "The crime in that novel was adultry and the perpetrator was The Reverend Mr. Dimmesdale, a clergyman.

"That's it, Bernadine. "When I was talking to Father Jack the other night he mentioned the book and that was it. As they say in the funny papers, everything fell in place."

Bernadine smiled. "But you will have to keep your voice down, Johnny. If Andrew Lloyd Weber hears about this he'll want to turn *The Scarlet Letter* into one of his musical plays and then he'll give it some title like *A Red Letter Day in Boston.*"

"We still have the mystery of why Graham asked Coral out on a date," said Blanche.

"That's no mystery," said Coral. "I asked him to."

*　　　*　　　*

John Badger Smith was now in the place he loved best to be, the classroom. Better than that, he was there to teach a class in modern poetry, more specifically T. S. Eliot's "The Waste Land." Even better yet, Mary, Bernadine and Blanche were sitting in the back of the room on extra chairs brought in by Doug Boito.

"Now does everyone have the three sheets of notes I passed out before vacation? Yes, Miss Peek, I do have an extra." Badger walked back to where Miss Peek was applying an emory board to her red nails. "Are we ready to begin?" He mounted the podium.

" 'The Waste Land' is a particularly appropriate poem to be studying at this time of year. Can someone tell me why? Donna."

"Because the time frame is Good Friday to Easter Sunday."

"Correct, Miss Lea. Eliot makes many literary and historical references to strengthen this time period. In fact, there are thirty-five different authors in many languages alluded to. Yes, Miss Peek?"

"Why does he do that? It's like that episode on 'Sybill' where she goes to confession and . . . . ."

"Congratulations, Carol. You have just made an allusion."

"I did?"

"You did." Under his breathe Badger said "Bless you, Miss Peek." Out loud he said, "You alluded to a television program you watch. Something you spend much time with, I believe. Eliot does the same thing. Where you allude to an episode in 'Sybill' on television, T. S. Eliot alludes to Shakespeare's The Tempest. "

"Why doesn't he allude to t.v. so we can understand him?"

Badger again blessed Miss Peek under his breath. "That would be fine today, but in a short time 'Sybill' will go into reruns and then be forgotten and become much more difficult to recognize than the Fisher King or any other of Eliot's references. Remember, poets read a great deal so make their allusions to what *they* know and love. That is one small part of the reason we study Eliot and others like him in the classroom. It wouldn't be necessary to study *Sybill* in class as the meanings are obvious, except perhaps for the allusion in the title.

Badger looked to the back of his classroom and the three smiling faces of Bernadine, Blanche, and Mary.

Outside the Door

In an artless room
of stone and steel
stands the old man of thirty
beating Emersonian virtues
on thirty drumless heads.

He does not know
a pie-eyed piper plays
in their hearts a minor key song
in a major mode.

THE END